Love to Thea, Al and Richard

10/24/12
To Meadow,
Thanks for your
great hands.

Jeffrey White

"Walking Through Walls is a fast and exciting read that delves into the psychology of survival and the culture of prison life. Winter's style makes you appreciate every character and consider how their behaviors are the product of multiple forces. Enjoyable and complex indeed, and highly recommended!"
—Joseph Gumina, Ph.D, Psychologist, San Francisco, CA

Also by Jeffrey Winters
Mystic Uncle & The Magical Bridge

Copyright © 2010 by Jeffrey Winters

All rights reserved. No part of this book may be reproduced or transmitted in any form or by any means, electronic or mechanical, including photocopying, recording, or by any information storage and retrieval system, without the written permission of the Publisher, except where permitted by law.

ISBN: 978-1-60594-615-3

Jeffrey Winters
701 Wisner Road,
Mount Shasta, CA 96067
(530) 926-5186
www.jeffreywinters.com
jeff@jeffreywinters.com

WALKING
THROUGH
WALLS

by Jeffrey Winters

CHAPTER 1

Waking up has gotten tougher. I lie in bed and watch my morning dream dissolve. Sometimes I feel as if I am active in my dream, while other times it seems as if something vague happened but I can't recall any details. I know when it's a bad dream, because I feel stiff in my body and slow in my head. At least three times a week, I wake up and feel the gut punch of losing my twin brother, who got blown up in that stupid mini war Desert Storm. When that happens, I tell myself to touch my heart and breathe deep. Rather then ruminate on my loss, I pull my sweatpants on and slump into the bathroom to pee. Afterwards, I look in the mirror. It's not time to pluck my eyebrow or put on lipstick. I'm thirty-eight—old enough to make a realistic assessment of my looks. Neither pretty nor ugly, just plain.

I brush my teeth and leave the prettying up for later. Right now I want my coffee. It's freshly brewed because I set the timer last night for six. It waits like a liquid lover, ready to bring me alive.

For sixteen years I was the business manager for an old-fashioned, caring internist. It was a small office—just me, the doctor, and our nurse, Juanita. I liked the job and respected the way my boss actually cared about our patients, and I really enjoyed Juanita, a no-nonsense gal who loved to laugh. Twice a week we would go out for dinner and a few beers. Our limited friendship means a lot to me.

My life is about to change radically. I feel as if I had walked into a storm and got blown into a parallel world. I'll be going to prison in a week. That scares me. I don't know if I can live locked up like an animal. I don't know if I have the strength or the self-discipline to conform. I don't know if I can become hard enough to tolerate the cruelty that prison breeds. Truth is, I don't know *shit* about life in prison except that it scares me to death. So, can I survive being behind bars? No one knows yet.

I might be ordinary, but I'm a good person, and the idea of sitting in a locked jail cell seems like a faraway nightmare. The thought that I did something bad enough to be put away makes me feel an unfamiliar shame. I wish my brother were alive and could guide me, help me, love me. He was always my protector, and now, without him, I'm more alone then ever.

I killed someone in a rage and what felt, at the time, like self-defense. My lawyer bargained it down from second-degree murder to involuntary manslaughter.

I can still hear the judge's words echo in my head: "You have been guilty of involuntary manslaughter. With good behavior, you can be out of prison in two and a half years."

CHAPTER 2

It was about four thirty in the morning and cold outside. I arrived at the prison in a white bus. I wore a maroon sweatshirt and could feel sweat under my pits.

I'm nervous—maybe *frightened* would be more accurate.

That first night, before locking me away, they put me into a room for a strip search. The room had one overhead light bulb, a metal door, and a big mirror on one wall. The guard, a tall brunette with long braids and oddly large, plump earlobes, had the broad, muscular back of a swimmer.

"Take off all your clothes," she said.

She put on rubber gloves, then started probing my orifices as if she were pushing quarters into a parking meter. She twisted my head up and around so I was forced to watch us in the mirror. Strapped on her belt were handcuffs, mace, and a big black stick. As she caught me staring at myself, a thin smile crossed her face, revealing pointed bottom teeth. She grinned at my humiliation. I tried to look down at the floor, but again she forced my face into the mirror. I felt the shame of no longer being the master of my own body.

What pissed me off the most, though, were the braids, which sweetened that otherwise brutal face. They seemed such a lie.

"You know why we search you?"

"No," I said. "Why?"

"Because you can have drugs or money or a cute little weapon up your pussy. You wouldn't believe what we pull out," she said, smirking in the mirror. I decided her eyes were dull gray, not dull blue.

She wanted to provoke me to squirm, scream, talk back, get angry. Her finger twisted inside me, and I suppressed a shudder of revulsion and fear.

I bent my head over my right shoulder to hide my face from my tormentor. "You're good at this," I said.

"You fucking with me?" she replied as her finger went another 180 degrees.

"Never."

"Good. Now, move on and pick up your uniform."

As I touched the blue denim pants and shirt, I had the unmistakable sensation of not getting enough air into my lungs. I had never had asthma, never come close to drowning, but in that moment, I couldn't breathe.

She looked at me and while her belly shook with laughter. "You little fuck, what a performance!" she said when she caught her breath. "You acting like I'm big and bad and hurting you, when all I have is love for you. Now, get out of here."

CHAPTER 3

After I put on the prison-issue blue jeans the first guard said, "Take her, Martha; I'm done."

Martha took my left arm and walked me through two steel gates, into the prison interior and down a walkway lined with cells. It was like walking down the painted cinder-block corridor of a cheap motel, except that these were metal bars, and everything—floor, walls, and ceiling—was a dismal, depressive gray. The noises and smells of fear and hostility were palpable, taut, like the muggy, static-charged air before a storm. My tongue felt dry, and my jaw clenched.

I remembered a scene from a *National Geographic* TV show. A bright-green viper struck a mouse, which staggered off a few steps and keeled over. The snake's tongue flickered, and then the mouth opened impossibly wide and slowly engulfed the mouse until it was just a big lump sliding inexorably down into the snake's belly. As I walked into the center of the cold, gray structure, I felt like some dead, limp creature being swallowed.

Martha, the guard who walked me to my cell, seemed to smell my fear. The other women prisoners must have, too. They hissed and laughed and jeered, "Welcome to the house of love, babe."

"Don't wet your pants," Martha said. "Not yet, anyway. Listen carefully to what I'm going to tell you. Don't get caught with drugs, make few friends, don't fight, but don't take any shit—ever.

If you're smart, you'll exercise when you can, or you'll blow up like a blimp eating this crap. Never diss your bunkie, or you might not wake up some morning. Love me like a sister, but don't show it or say anything. You understand what I'm telling you?"

"Yes."

"Good. One more thing. I know what goes on in this place. I have friends on both sides of the denim. Don't approach me for help. You need help, talk to your bunkie—she knows how to reach me. That's it for now."

She stopped at a cell and opened the door with the sort of big, round keys I'd seen in old prison movies. Inside was a tiny room with two narrow cots. I wondered how a fat person could possibly sleep on one without sagging off the edge. There was a sink and a plastic wall mirror so small you could see only a piece of your face in it. A small writing table of dull gray metal filled the corner. The bars on the door were as thick as my wrist.

As the door clanged shut behind me, a black woman in her mid-thirties looked up from the far cot. At this miserable hour of five thirty a.m., she was already dressed.

"Hello," I managed to say, staring into compelling black eyes that sparkled like obsidian.

"You staring at your new bunkie?" she snapped.

"No, no. Sorry, I didn't—"

"Don't apologize so quick. And tell me what you're staring at."

"Your eyes, they're amazing—so dark and shiny."

"You battin' for the other side?" A look of disgust crossed her face.

"No, are you?" I quipped, then instantly regretted it.

"You being cute with me? I *live* for my boneyard visits."

"What's that?"

"A conjugal visit with my husband, once every four months, in a little cabin on the other side of prison—one hour."

"That enough time?"

"It's never enough time when you want it to last."

"I'm Nina," I said. I tried looking her in the face again, but my eyes fell.

"I'm June." She looked me up and down. Though she seemed relaxed, she had an inner intensity that made me feel nervous and exposed. I hated the feeling.

"You been in here long?"

"Three years, with one to go. You don't look like you been around this house before."

"No, never been in a prison."

"Well, you're in a swamp now, and you could survive, get eaten, or end up crazy."

"Thanks for the scare."

"It's not about being scared. It's about staying alive, so you don't end up depressed and a love hustler to some gang motherfucking asshole. This is serious, what I'm trying to tell you."

"What kind of gang?"

"Watch out for Alice," she replied.

"Who's Alice?"

"She's not a person. Alice is all the white punks. The Aryan sisters into pain and hate. They love new white girls—not quite blond, innocent and scared, ready to hide in their tit." She paused, then added, "They love tattoos. Most in here do. But these Aryan bitches are about as dumb and ruthless as it gets. They enjoy giving and receiving pain. Makes them feel alive. They're twisted, and the most twisted one is always the leader."

"Why are you telling me all this?" I asked.

"When I came here, my new bunkie did the same for me. She took my naive mind and taught me how to survive. Call this payback."

"I don't know what to say."

"Good. Don't say anything—just listen up. Here's a few dry facts: This prison houses about five hundred women. Most are in for assault, some murder, mostly robbery. Recently a lot more white-collar crime, accountants and bookkeepers embezzling company funds." June paused, looked at me thoughtfully, and continued.

"At first you can't trust anyone—maybe not even me. The good news is, the prison authorities try to remove the really violent women who'd disturb the harmony of this shit house. But it would be a mistake to think they're successful. That's why you could easily get killed here for showing disrespect to the wrong person. Violence and the fear of violence are as ordinary as eating. You can see it and smell it. Do you understand what I'm trying to tell you?"

"Yeah. This place is dangerous, and I should watch out."

"Good. Now I'm going to read. Not a stupid romance so I can rub myself—it's history.

I glanced at her book. It was about Eleanor Roosevelt. "Why do you read about her," I ask.

"She reminds me of my mom: smart, strong, and serious. My mom became frail like Eleanor as she got older, but you never saw any weakness, only tremendous energy. Don't ever underestimate me, either," she added, darting me a serious glare.

"I won't," I stammered. "Promise."

June reached over to the small shelf above her cot and took down a worn hardcover book, then flopped down on her stomach with her head propped back just inches from the book. She never looked up at me or said another word—just stayed in that position like a dark goddess frozen in place. All of a sudden, a shrill, harsh whistle went off.

CHAPTER 4

"Let's go," June ordered. "Now, listen, I'm only gonna tell you this once. Walk behind me. In here, that shows respect. You have soft brown hair. Women like to touch soft hair. Nice body—small tits, but firm. Your face is ordinary, but I like the little blush in your cheeks. Women will notice you. Go to the food line and always look straight ahead. Don't do that dumb stare like you did with me. When you stare like a deer, they think you're an easy slave. That's their excuse to handle you. No one'll touch you this soon. They'll talk lots of trash, though. Let it melt off you like a snowflake. Food sucks, but better eat it. It beats hunger. Don't sit with me yet; they'll think you burn coal."

"What's that?" I asked.

"It means you're doing a black. Someone asks you something, answer quietly, look them in their face real quick, then be quiet. Lot of girls get in trouble because they can't shut up. Women here will use your words—twist 'em, play with you. Mind shit. Try not to play. Got it?"

Suddenly, a strong visual memory entered my mind: my twin brother, Donny, before he went off to fight in Desert Storm. He was in uniform and nervous. I hugged him, and he sucked in a deep breath, looked at me, and exhaled through puckered lips, slowly blowing the breath away. That breath was all he needed to say.

Taking a deep breath like Donny's to quiet my fear, I looked up at June and said, "Got it."

The doors opened automatically, and I tensed the way I used to at the high whine of the dentist's drill.

The gray walls of the dining room reminded me of a five-day rain in late fall. The guards in their brown uniforms looked mean, and the inmates, in blue denim, had their attitudes pasted on their faces: frightened, vicious, or vacant. This place was a manmade cave, designed to make you feel like a bug. Food in metal trays. Some people talking, others just looking down.

When June and I entered the dining room, a lot of eyes stared at me. I got in line cafeteria-style with a plastic tray and a plastic fork and avoided everyone's eyes.

When I passed one woman, she touched my shoulder. I looked at her face. She had painted her lips with dark purple that reached almost into her nostrils. She said, "You need bud or crank, let me know."

"Okay," I said, and moved straight ahead. In front of me, I saw mustard-colored scrambled eggs that looked as if they were growing fungus. A big, muscular inmate with a snake tattoo on her wrist slapped a spoonful onto my plate. "You want more, ask your mama," she taunted.

Moving on to the greasy shredded potatoes, I tossed them over the eggs. Next, I was allowed two pieces of white bread that looked like putty. At the end of the counter, I got coffee—bitter as gall, and no sugar. I rubbed my tongue back and forth on the roof of my mouth, but that only spread the bitterness around.

I made for a half-full table in the corner. Five women sat eating and talking. I sat on the end. June walked over to some friends, a racial mix that included two Asian women. Somehow, I had expected everyone to hang out with their own kind. Maybe I'd seen too many prison movies.

I sat down, and my mood shifted from being a wary observer to feeling sorry for myself. I wanted to pinch myself on the thigh the way I had done as a girl when I did something stupid. I glanced around at all these strange women in prison drabs, and my heart thudded.

A deep, strong voice blasted me out of my self-pity. "Honey, you gonna eat this rubber, you got to stop staring at it."

The unlikely source of the brawny voice was a skinny woman with a freckled, farm-girl face.

"I can't eat this stuff," I said.

"Oh, yeah, you can," she boomed, sitting down next to me.

"I'm Wilma. I gotta tell you something."

"I'm listening," I said, following my bunkie's instructions and looking into her eyes, then back down at the unappetizing glop on my tray.

"You're new. I saw you in line, looking like a little puppy. Get it: we don't *dine* here. No one brings you red wine to wash down the steak. You have to bypass your taste buds. It takes effort, but it can be done."

"How?" I said, knowing she'd tell me even if I didn't ask.

"Ever watch a Chink eat a bowl of rice? They don't lift it to their mouths—they shovel it down the chute, and never mind chewing."

She stuck her plastic spoon under a jiggling mound of eggs. "Here—watch this. You could eat wet feathers this way if you had to."

Lifting the spoon to her mouth, she sucked the food off it and swallowed.

"That's how you eat this crap. Hop it over your taste buds and you won't puke on everybody. Do this for a couple of weeks until it doesn't matter anymore. You get so you can do it without chewing. I know it's dog shit, but you gotta eat."

I had to smile—getting a lecture on how to eat. It reminded me of my brother eating boiled fish at our grandmother's house when we were kids. He would pretend he was going to vomit.

"Thanks, I'll remember that."

"Don't thank people so fast," she snapped. "It puts you in debt. Now you owe me. Not much, but you still owe me. Someday, I might want a magazine you've got. I'll be easy on you. But don't say thanks for every miserable fucking piece of advice somebody throws your way." Wilma got up and carried her tray to another table, where she sat down with a few women and began laughing. They looked over at me, and I knew that my eating lesson was the morning joke.

The next morning when the doors were opened, we had half an hour to shower, use the toilet, and get ready for the day. June was there ahead of me.

"You stink from nerves," she said. "Go shower and shit. Come on, I'll show you."

I followed her, respectfully, to the communal bathroom. A row of toilets lined the walls. They had partitions between the stalls, but no doors. Anyone walking in could see you sitting there wiping your ass. I would have to get over my squeamishness in a hurry.

The showers were set to run for one hour. You waited for an available showerhead and rushed in. Soap and shampoo hung in plastic containers attached to the wall. The shower scene reminded me of high school gym—bodies standing close enough to touch naked skin on either side of you.

I ducked under an open showerhead. Someone pinched my ass, and several naked women giggled. I quickly lathered my pits and my ass so I could rinse off, then washed my hair in record time. We were handed a towel and expected to get out of there fast. I put on my denims and left.

Clean and ready to go. I was caught up in getting it right—no time to be nervous.

CHAPTER 5

The next day, I had my teeth checked by an old dentist with tufts of black hair on his knuckles. As he probed, his knuckle hair rubbed against my gums, like a hairy spider moving around in my mouth. He had yellow teeth, and beer on his breath. When he said, "You have good strong teeth," I wanted to gag, but I was learning to stuff my revulsion.

After the dental exam, a guard took me to an office, where three other guards were drinking coffee. They were big, burly women with batons, stun guns, and handcuffs on their belts. Two had tattoos on their arms. One guard walked by as if she owned the place and, if a truck got in her way, she'd rather shoot the driver than get out of the way. These were the zookeepers. And we were the critters.

The sergeant gave me the usual once-over, up and down. She reminded me of a documentary on wolves I saw once, where the alpha female would pee to mark her territory. The sergeant used her gaze to remind me of just where I stood in her pack.

"You worked in a doctor's office," she said by way of introduction. "So you've been assigned to work with the doctor, cleaning up the infirmary records." She belched, and the other two chuckled. "You caught a good job. Report to the infirmary in ten minutes." And she brushed me away as if I were a bothersome fly.

The other guard escorted me to the infirmary, where they wanted me to create and organize a filing system. The oblong room had two empty metal beds, a small stainless steel sink, and a table strewn with loose files and a worn wraparound blood-pressure gauge. A stethoscope hung from the loop in the venetian blind cord.

I watched a patient come and go. The doctor was quick. I could see how it worked. He examined an inmate and treated her for whatever ailment had brought her to his office, and she got put on a list, but there was no history file of any kind. That lack of documentation meant that only the doctor knew what was going on with the patient, or what he *thought* was going on. If he left the prison, it would be impossible for the next doctor to pick up the case without starting over. I enjoyed organizing and making files, so this work assignment was my first shred of anything that felt like luck.

He walked out. The only other person in the room was a timid-looking woman with a teenager's face. She approached me with rubber gloves and bleach and, in a shy voice, told me to scrub the walls. She didn't offer me a mask to protect me from the acrid bleach fumes. As I scrubbed walls caked with years of cigarette smoke, I decided that anyone forced to stay in the infirmary had probably died from secondhand smoke.

The doctor came in as I was finishing with the first wall. He had gray hair and a big belly and exuded the faint smell of barbecue.

"Not an easy job," he said, looking away as if suddenly distracted by something.

"How long have you been here?" I asked.

"Too long—maybe sixteen years," he said.

"Wow."

He looked over at me as if I had said something profound.

"I only come here for two hours every Monday, Wednesday, and Friday," he said.

Then he looked right at me. "You know what I do?" Without

waiting for an answer, he said, "I try to keep everyone happy."

It didn't take long to figure out how Dr. Feelgood "kept everyone happy": by trading drugs for sex with inmates. Walking into the back office, I saw him leaning back, eyes rolled upward, getting a blow job. Linda, a petite Asian woman who looked to be in her sixties, turned her head slightly without breaking her rhythm and winked at me. I left the room and said nothing to anyone.

The next day, Linda, the woman who serviced him, explained that he wrote prescriptions for Ritalin, codeine cough syrup, Valium, amphetamines, and other drugs, using the names of his regular patients. He then had his nurse pick up the drugs from the pharmacy, and he would distribute them inside the prison. This man's conduct was completely foreign to me. He was sleazy, to be sure, but for whatever reason, I decided he was harmless.

CHAPTER 6

The second night, I ate dinner at a table of inmates who were silent and seemed to have no friends or affiliations with any particular ethnic group. They sat with shoulders slumped, as if they were extras in a movie about depressed people in a hospital facility. The inmates at the other tables were rowdy and noisy.

Later, I walked into the TV room. A small TV sat in the corner, surrounded by cheap plastic waiting-room chairs. Tables were set up for playing cards or doing crossword puzzles. Two guards circled the room slowly, like lions looking for the weak or lame antelope in the herd. The room was creepy. A heavy-set guard walked past an anorexic, junkie-faced prisoner and stepped on her foot. The prisoner bit her lip. The guard softly grabbed her earlobe and whispered into her ear, and the woman made a childlike moan.

"'C'mere," June called out from a nearby table. She was playing cards with two other women. In the background, I could hear the canned laughter from an *I Love Lucy* rerun. I walked to June's table and sat down.

"Don't stare at that cruel shit," June hissed.

"What's going on?

"Welcome to prison life, you old virgin," June's friend chuckled, and then whooped like someone who had just found a hundred-dollar bill on the street.

"Why you in?" June's friend asked. I hesitated.

"My name's Edie. Go on, tell me what got you in this dump."

Like it or not, her question pushed me to center stage. But at least it was a distraction from all that was going on around me. The tight, claustrophobic feeling in my chest cavity loosened. From the moment I had entered this place, my breath was shallow, and I constantly had that scared, sweaty smell. But now I noticed I wasn't scared talking with these women. Even the knot in my chest began to relax.

"I killed a woman and plea-bargained down to involuntary manslaughter," I said.

"No shit—you don't look much like you could kill anybody."

"Why'd you kill her?" June asked.

"Honey, might as well make this good," said the second card player. "We ain't going no place." Her name was Lorraine, and she had to tip the scales at over two hundred. She had a scar shaped like a question mark across her cheek, one tooth missing and the rest full of gold. *This one's been through it,* I thought. And yet, her expression was warm and curious. "C'mon, honey, tell us your story."

I lifted my head. They looked at me, and June pushed her jaw out and her head went up. I knew she was telling me to go ahead.

"I was working in a doctor's office," I said. "My Peruvian friend Juanita worked there, too. She was a nurse and I was the assistant. She helped me run the place for a family doctor—nice guy, really cared. His patients mattered to him; it wasn't just about the money."

"Yeah, yeah—and?" Edie said.

"Don't rush her," Lorraine growled.

June took charge. "Just tell it slow, Nina. Don't leave anything out, girl. The cards can wait; we' don't exactly have a busy schedule."

"Okay, so Juanita and I got to be good friends. I could trust her."

"Why can't it be that easy to trust a man?" Edie muttered.

"Go on—what happened?" Lorraine asked.

"One Tuesday night around six thirty, we were alone, putting files away. Juanita was in the examining room making sure all the drugs and equipment were locked up. We were almost done, talking about going out for food and a beer." I paused, and their fixed gazes compelled me to continue. "We heard a knock on the door, and a woman's voice asked us to open up. I figured it was one of the other gals from the next office. I open the door, and this young white couple in their twenties, maybe early thirties, walks in. She's wearing a dark green cashmere coat. Expensive. She had big round gold earrings and dark red lipstick. He had on a strange blue silk scarf. They were right out of a magazine ad, dripping money but both with druggie-stupid stares."

June looked around the table and said, "Sounds like they were dressed for the big party. Why such big earrings? I never liked how big, heavy earrings felt. Go on."

The three women laid their cards down, so I went on. "They walk in and close the door. Juanita comes out of the room just as I'm about to ask what they want. The man looks back at the entry door and kicks it shut behind him, then pulls out a little pistol. His eyes were tiny little slits.

"'We want your drugs'", he says. His voice was cracked, and I could see he was scared.

He looks at Juanita, who's still in her white uniform. The woman he's with screams, '"You fat piece of shit, where do you keep the narcotics? Quick, tell me!'"

Lorraine slammed her right hand on the table, startling me and getting a stink-eye from one of the guards: "Strung-out rich white motherfuckers with their suburban junk habit. Who does that bitch think she's callin' fat? Me, I woulda stuck a pencil in her eye."

Edie nodded vigorously. "See? Those fuckin' gold earrings! Shit, where do these miserable punks get their money?" Then Edie turned to me, shifting to the polite, upbeat voice of a hostess in an upscale restaurant. "Honey, please continue." She hadn't missed a beat, and focused her attention completely on me.

"At first, I was more confused than scared," I said. "Juanita had been robbed before, and she spoke slowly and seriously. She told them there were no hard drugs in the office—just aspirin, antibiotics, stuff like that. 'Fuck that—you lie!' the woman shrieked."

"So, what did they do?" June asked.

She screamed at him really loud. He bobbed his head as though he was waking up from a dream, then pointed a pistol in slow motion with the same blank stare . . . and shot Juanita point-blank. I thought she was hit in the chest and would die. Then he walked out without saying anything. He never even looked back at his partner."

"Fuckin' coward," June breathed.

"What the bitch do?" Lorraine was shaking her head.

"Just looked at me. Juanita had her hand on her right side; blood was spilling out through her fingers. She slid to the ground, whispering, 'I'll be okay.'

"Thinking she was going to die, I looked at the woman in the fancy coat and just felt this cold rage. My mind snapped. I had no idea if she had a weapon, but I knew my life was in danger. I stepped up to this miserable woman's face, remembering what my brother, Donny, had taught me from his martial arts training when we were in high school: If you're in physical danger, punch 'em in the throat.

"Good move." Lorraine nodded at me.

"So what'd you do?" Edie asked.

"I grabbed her hair, pulled her head back almost to her shoulder. When her neck was exposed, I chopped her in the throat. She tried to scream. Then, I bent my fingers and rammed the knuckles into her throat. She made a gurgling sound. Then I grabbed her head, pulled it towards me so I could yank her earring off—it ripped right through her ear."

"Ooh, girl, that hurt," Lorraine crooned. "You got you some

bad-ass moves."

I didn't respond, wiping my forehead with the back of my hand. Sweat dripped down my cheeks as I relived the memory of that night.

"She gasped and moaned like an asthmatic trying to catch her breath. I couldn't stop. I hit her in the throat again. Juanita pleaded with me to stop, but I wasn't hearing her. It felt like riding a wild horse that I couldn't get off. I hit her again. She collapsed on the floor and died—I'd broken her windpipe."

Edie looked at me. "Shit, girl, you got some kind of bad-ass demon inside you."

Lorraine was bending her fingers and hitting the coffee cup. June's eyes were turned upward as if she'd spotted a spider web on the ceiling. "Are you *nuts*?" she finally said.

"I don't know. I thought Juanita was going to die. I remember thinking that someone was taking my friend from me. And I remembered my brother getting killed. I exploded. I felt strange, as if somebody else was acting in my place. But I can still feel my knuckles hitting that throat—the way it kind of crunched and gave—and me not being able to stop."

The three women sat in silence for several minutes. Finally, Lorraine picked up her cards. "Damn, that's a good story. What happened to that little motherfucking coward with the cap gun?"

"The police tracked him down to his house. They arrested him. He hired a famous lawyer, who got him off with drug rehab in a country-club prison."

June looked concerned. "What about your friend—she make it?"

"Yeah, she lived. The bullet almost ruined the use of her right arm, though. A team of surgeons repaired it. She'll never be the same, but she made it."

"You still talk?" Edie asked.

"She moved back to Peru. She sent me a postcard, that's about it."

"Sounds like self-defense to me. How you sentenced?" Edie asked.

"The woman had no weapons I could see, but could have been trying to kill me. I know I felt I was acting in self-defense. But the prosecutor claimed I hit her repeatedly with malicious intent. He said it was involuntary manslaughter The judge agreed and gave me four years—out in two and a half if I behave myself."

"You got fucked!" June said.

"We *all* got fucked," Lorraine said. "Not really the point anymore, is it. We're just here in this shit-hole hotel." Her face turned pensive. "I like how you fought that bitch, knuckles bent. Have to remember that. Good move."

"Ever feel guilty?" Edie asked.

"It's strange," I said. "I never hurt anyone in my life. But no, I don't feel guilt. I thought she was going to kill me."

"Remember, Nina," June warned. "Women here don't care why you're in. They see a white girl hanging with blacks, some white bitches don't like that. Worse, we have one really bad Chicana and two Nazi chicks who might fuck with you. Watch your ass."

"You play gin rummy?" Edie asked.

"Yeah," I said.

"Deal her in," said Lorraine.

CHAPTER 7

As a child, I never thought about time—there was always plenty of right now to occupy me. I had tender memories of each season. My breath would chill in fall; in winter, Mom would bring me soup after I came in from playing in the snow; the family took country drives in spring; and I always got plenty of mosquito bites—and sometimes poison ivy—in summer.

Two weeks before entering prison, I had my thirty-eighth birthday. Somewhere between thirty-five and forty, I had begun to notice time. It started flying by—I was on a speeding train, plunging through life, with an occasional whistle stop at an unmarked station. I thought I could get off the train, but never managed to long enough to gain perspective on what I was doing or feeling in my life.

In prison, time took on a completely new dimension. Each day bled into the next as my world shrank. I saw the same cage, uniforms, and faces, same toilet, same food, same hustles, same old routines. It felt like being in a TV set with only one channel. I watched this woman at dinner who looked as if patience was what the devil required of her. So she had this eternally blank, indifferent stare as if she had already lost her memory. Another gal was the poster child for despair, with crooked lines coming down off each side of her mouth, like on a talking puppet, and eyes the yellow-brown of half-dried dog shit. I heard the metal clang as they shut my cell door, and saw the same lights go out at the same time every night. In the morning, the same toilets and shower. The line for food. All of it ticked like a huge second hand on an invisible clock. All the ticks felt like Novocain as my mind made the adjustment to prison time.

Also, with so few windows, there's little sun, so the dull gray surroundings made my brain forget about color and vibrancy and sparks of energy. I began to look at those gray concrete floors and see if I could find a crack. I would look at the lumpy mashed potatoes and visualize cotton candy.

Prison routine, conformity of action, and constant fear had an immediate effect on me. After three weeks, the isolation from everything I'd ever known tore through me. It's not the same as being lonely or shy, where you keep to yourself on the outside. This internal isolation was the place where I hid while my mind quietly split and splintered.

Here, instead of a tree-filled park, I was surrounded by women who were angry, disgraced, or deathly sad. This environment shifted my focus from the external to the internal, as if a flashlight were shining on sections of my mind that had always rested in darkness.

Before prison, I had a routine. Sometimes it was like being in a time warp. I'd wake up, pee, drink coffee, go to work, pee, eat lunch, work till quitting time, go home, watch TV, go to bed. The same routine every day, with little room for joy or love. Occasionally, I'd take a walk through Golden Gate Park—my antidote for the deadening sameness.

When the lights went out at night, I stared up at the dark. Vivid memories of my past surfaced as if I were watching them on a movie screen. In my precriminal life, I didn't chew on my memories. I wasn't concerned with inner thoughts and feelings. I didn't ponder; I just moved mechanically through my life.

In prison, I began to observe my thoughts and memories as if they were a story about another person. I began to review my life and think about events and decisions I had made before landing in prison. Sometimes, a pattern would emerge; other times, my life path seemed random. Looking with detachment at these memories, I was like a potter considering a chunk of new clay before placing it on a wheel.

One overwhelming realization surfaced over and over again: I was getting nowhere in life. I was a machine, a robot, operating without enthusiasm. Seeing myself as a disengaged player, turning the wheel of life, was horrifying. I was dying and didn't even know it. I couldn't help thinking of the Everly Brothers song "Wake Up, Little Susie."

I suppose the mind can be tuned in prison, but mostly I saw it sicken and rot. I was lost. I wasn't sure which path my mind would follow—until my past started to catch up with me.

CHAPTER 8

When I was born, my parents argued about names. They settled on Nina. My brother, Donny, was their firstborn, and I was his fraternal twin sister. We were the Waldovsky twins, and everyone on the south side of Milwaukee praised my mother's fertility.

It was a blue-collar neighborhood of Polish and Lithuanian immigrants. Whole families worked in the local breweries, where the smell of hops saturated the air.

My dad was a mechanic who could fix any car on the road. My mother met him in 1950, when she drove into his shop to get her Pontiac Bonneville a new water pump. They began to talk, and from the way both told it, they fell in love right then and never fell out.

It was a chancy union, because Mom was Jewish and Dad was Catholic. Mom was a little bitty woman, maybe four feet eleven, with golden hair and soft, delicate hands. Her complexion was pale except for a vivid red spot above each cheek that made it look as if she were blushing for no reason. Dad was tall and thin, with strong, sinewy muscles. I loved to be hugged by him and feel his physical strength. He smiled easily, and people were comfortable around him. My parents made a good-looking couple.

My mom's mother wasn't happy with the marriage. Mom's father had come over from Warsaw, Poland. As a teenager, Grandpa Lou hated the way the Catholics bullied the Jewish kids, so he became a boxer as well as a religious man.

I visited him on cold days, when the temperatures hovered around eighteen degrees, and I can still see him outside wearing only a light T-shirt. With that thick neck, his face reminded me of a bulldog's. My dad would call him Tough Lou because he once grabbed an anti-Semite bully by the shoulders, picked him up like a bag of potatoes, and threw him into the wall of an old brick building. Grandpa Lou was very loving to my brother and me. When Grandpa met my dad, they would talk for hours, drinking beer and enjoying each other's company. It mattered to him that my dad was honest and would take care of his daughter.

My parents celebrated Christmas and Easter. Our entire family went over to Grandpa Lou and Nana's for the Passover, and when we were older, they took my brother and me to the synagogue to celebrate the Jewish High Holidays.

Donny and I never developed much interest in religion. I didn't like the images of a skinny, bloodied, sad Jesus. I was told he died for my sins, but come on, I didn't do anything bad enough for someone to die over.

In synagogue, they prayed in Hebrew. We never knew what they were talking about. Some of the melodies were beautiful, but the rest of the service was alien and remote.

My parents never pushed us to go to church or synagogue. They didn't mind our apathy toward religion. What did matter to them was that we be self-reliant and responsible. Donny and I always believed we should take care of each other, and knowing he was my protector brought me tremendous comfort.

When Donny and I went into seventh grade, we began playing with the new friends who came to this huge three-story red brick building. Many of the kids were from different parts of Milwaukee. The school was harsh and reminded me of underground tunnels with dim lighting. I remember that the bathroom had little black and white tiles and very high windows. The far stall always smelled from the cigarettes of a group of girls who liked acting tough. Other girls would stand in front of the mirror putting on different shades of lipstick and fussing with their hair.

Even then it seemed that Donny was the aggressive one and I was just a notch above being shy. In ninth grade, Donny went out for the wrestling team and made first string in his weight division. He loved to fight. Grandpa Lou had been teaching him to box, and now he was on the wrestling team. My best friend, Sarah, and I would watch Donny when he had a match at our school. Sometimes my mom and dad would come. Watching him fight, I felt nervous and, at the same time, excited. When he won a match, I would yell and scream.

One time Donny lost a match to a black kid from the other side of town. This kid was so fast, Donny didn't have a chance to use his moves. He was in the locker room afterward and heard "nigger" jokes for the first time. Donny didn't like what they were saying, and he left. At an early age, and because of the influence of our parents and grandparents, we didn't hold people's difference from us against them. Instead, Donny left school that day and ran into the guy who beat him. He went over to him, nodded his head, and just said, "Great match." Then he laughed and said, "Wish it was the other way around."

"Thanks," the guy replied. "You know, man, you were just half a second too slow. Next time it might be your turn."

"Do you know how to box?" Donny asked.

"My brother came back from the army in Japan," the guy said. "He's teaching me some wild stuff they call karate. It has ways of fighting you wouldn't believe. Interested?"

"Yeah. My name's Donny. Just tell me where and when."

"I'm Billy. My brother's teaching a few guys at two o'clock on Saturday in our garage. Know how to get to Benson Street? It's on the other side of town."

"Not for sure," Donny said, "but I've got a map. What's the address and I'll be there."

"Two thirty-six Benson Street. Two this Saturday. He doesn't like it if you're late."

Donny put his hand out and they shook. I remember this story because it influenced my life. For the next four years, Donny became a student of Billy's brother and practiced Japanese-style karate. He also became good friends with Billy. He had other friends in school, too, of course, but his friendship with Billy and learning karate were special to him—he shared it with me, not them.

I was on the girls' volleyball team. I wasn't bad, but I was never really a good athlete. I just enjoyed playing on a team.

Sometimes Donny came home all excited about what he was learning in Billy's garage. He wanted to show me some moves and practice on me. He was gentle, but I didn't really want to get thrown to the ground or twisted up like a pretzel. So Donny decided he would teach me some very basic things a girl needed to know to protect herself. He had me practice hitting the throat a thousand times, so I could stop an attacker dead if I had to.

In our senior year of high school, my other close friend, Nancy, got pregnant. She came from a strict Catholic family, and it looked as if they might kick her out of the house. My mom took her in, and we all sat up with her while she cried. We listened and felt bad for her. In those days, a Catholic girl wouldn't consider an abortion, and being a single mom was a huge taboo. Her boyfriend stepped up and asked her to marry him. It was forced, I could tell—a daytime soap opera with people I actually knew. As the years went on, though, Nancy kept her marriage together. She and her husband had eight kids and shared a rare commodity: they still loved each other.

Donny broke up with his girlfriend in our senior year. I wasn't dating, so my brother and I started hanging out again. We would often get a burger and go to a movie on the weekend. We joked how people thought we were on a date. But this was better than a date. I loved my brother to the bones, and I knew how much he cared about me. Being together as family felt more natural and comfortable than anything else in the world. We went bowling a lot (a big

Milwaukee activity), and then over to Billy's house for dinner with his family. My favorite memory was during the Christmas holidays, when we would drive down to Chicago to buy presents for our parents. Chicago made Milwaukee seem like a dinky little town, and we walked around staring up at the tall buildings until our feet hurt. I felt strong, happy, and good. I loved being with my brother.

Even though it was my last year of high school, I felt no hurry to hook up with a boy. The guys in school seemed younger than I, and fixated on sex. I had decided that making love with someone was special—something that could wait for my true love. I just wasn't eager to try it out with a boy I didn't really love.

One fond recollection was how my dad loved Carvel ice cream that came out of a machine, all soft and swirly. It became a family tradition to get some after dinner on Friday nights. Those were wonderful days.

CHAPTER 9

When Donny graduated from high school, he joined the army to fight in Desert Storm. A year later, at the age of nineteen, he was killed in the desert, surrounded by hot sand dunes. It was supposed to be a quick little war, but an artillery shell killed him.

Steven, Donny's best friend in the army, was wounded in the same action that killed Donny. When he finished his rehab, he came to visit our family, to share our sorrow and bring some black-and-white pencil sketches Donny had drawn when he wasn't fighting in the field.

When I found out that Donny was dead, part of me went numb. It seemed as if an empty cavern formed around my heart. With his death, part of me got erased.

Steven was from Wyoming. I already knew from Donny's letters what close friends they had become. My first impression of him was his rugged looks. When we were alone in the den, he cried on my shoulder, then held me while I wept. After dinner with Mom and Dad, Steven asked if he and I could be alone. We went upstairs to Donny's bedroom. Looking around at the football posters, Steven told me Donny had saved the lives of many men before the explosion.

He said, "Nina, as Donny was dying, he asked that you and I do something for him."

"What?" I asked.

"We had a Jewish buddy from Baltimore. The three of us were a team. When Larry got killed, both Donny and I heard the rabbi say a strange-sounding prayer over his body in Hebrew. Donny went over and asked what the prayer was called. The rabbi said it was called *kaddish*—a very old prayer for the dead." It had haunted me.

Suddenly, Steven began to cry again. I looked at this man who had lost his two best buddies. I held him again, and we rocked back and forth, both in pain. Finally, he wiped his eyes and continued.

"I held Donny's head right before he died. He looked up at me and moved his mouth slowly, asking if you and I would recite kaddish for him. 'The Jew in me is proud,' he said."

It was amazing to share a spiritual connection with Steven as I grieved. I knew it wasn't a coincidence that Donny had provided me with the comfort of his best friend—even in death he was trying to protect me.

Steven took out a piece of paper and said, "I went to the chaplain, who had a copy of this prayer in English for the Jewish soldiers." Steven showed me the paper and held it in front of us as we began to recite kaddish:

> *"Yis-ga-dal v'yis-ka-dash sh'may ra-bo*
> *B'ol-mo dee-v'ro chir-u-say, v'yam-leech mal-chu-say,*
> *B'cha-yay-chon uv-yo-may-chon, uv-cha-yay d'chol Bays yis-ro-ayhl,*
> *Ba a-go-lo u'viz'man ko-reev, v'im-ru Omayn."*

We recited the entire prayer in Donny's bedroom. The Hebrew sounds reached deep into my soul. I looked up and cried, "I miss you, brother. I love you and I miss you."

Steven sat silently by my side. We stood up together and went downstairs. My mother was sitting on the sofa holding her box of elegant glass miniatures. For years she had created small glass figures, selling them to an upscale store in Chicago. In the box were the pieces she would never sell. She picked out one of a boy standing over a new car. It was Donny with his first car. She asked Steven if he would honor the family by keeping the figurine. Steven took my mom's hand. He stared at the glass miniature of Donny, and a smile came over his face.

Steven gently put the figurine on the table. "Mrs. Waldovsky..." He paused to contain his tears, then reached over and hugged my mother. She put her arms around him. My father had been very quiet. Steven went over to him and hugged him with tremendous strength. My father put his arms around Steven and almost picked him up in the air. When they broke apart, Steven said, "Donny was my brother. I loved him. God bless him." Then he held both my mother's and father's hands with gentle dignity. I'll never forget that afternoon.

Even though I think about Donny often, something new started to develop once I was behind bars. His memory became crisp and resonated within me with a new, deep force and clarity. I had an urge to talk with Donny and felt as if he could hear me. "Brother, I need help in this place," I began. "Be my angel protector. Donny, I love and miss you. Help me.... I'm scared."

I told him how proud I was of his bravery and heroism, and I let him know how alone I felt without him. When I finished talking to him, a calm came over me, and a familiar voice said, "My dear sister, I am here for you."

CHAPTER 10

It only took four months for me to fall almost effortlessly into a routine. While working in the infirmary, I created a color-coded filing system: blue dots for chronic illness, red ones for one-time visits, green ones for prescriptions. Each file showed time, date, and dosage—basic stuff.

Occasionally, I'd hear Doc moaning from the back office, and once I blundered in while he was having sex. There's no question that you miss being touched in such a sterile environment, but watching the doctor grunting and flopping like a beached whale on top of a woman was hardly stimulating. Their bodies flailed about, and catching a glimpse of his dainty pink erection was no more interesting than watching toast pop out of a toaster.

Once the doc knew I wouldn't service him, he chose to confide in me instead. It was another misplaced intimacy, but he needed to talk candidly and trust someone. The fact that he chose me to trust did upgrade my prison experience from zombie to something approaching human. It sounds silly maybe, but I was grateful. The trust he placed in me mattered, I suppose, because trust was largely absent in this place. He began by telling me about his life, starting with his late wife, whom he described as his first and only love.

"What happened to her?" I asked.

"Ovarian cancer happened."

"I'm sorry," I said.

"She was fifty-six when she died. We had a good life together. Truth is, I've never gotten over losing her companionship. My entire life I've been awkward with women, but with her there was only ease and love. It was remarkable. . . . I miss it."

"You seem to do all right with the women in here," I said without any judgment.

He sighed. "What's going on, Nina, is something that literally fell into my lap. One day I was treating a prisoner for serious arthritis in her knee joints. She nonchalantly opened my zipper, and the rest is history."

I blushed.

"I didn't mean to embarrass you," he said. "I just wanted to explain that I am careful about who I choose to have sex with, and I don't overdo the drug prescribing. I'm careful, and I cover my tracks."

"Do you deal heavy drugs?" I asked.

"Ritalin is so overprescribed, it's a cinch for me to get it. Same with Valium. I never barter with heavy drugs like coke or heroin. Some milder pain pills, maybe. Listen, I select who I have this arrangement with. For instance, I don't have anything to do with gang members or violent women."

Doc looked old and tired. It was strangely dreamlike, listening while he discussed his sexual partners.

"I like most of the women here," he said. "Most of the time they're treated like animals on the outside and worse on the inside. I'll give the inmates medical care when they need it. The gatekeepers of this place told me just to give them an aspirin and send them back. The reality is, many of these women have been medically neglected for years. If I can help them, I will."

Later I spoke with the older Asian woman, Anna. She told me that the inmates who were his drug whores enjoyed the old man. He was gentle and appreciated the sex, and so did they. Also, anyone with access to drugs had power. They could barter for cigarettes, obtain favors, command respect.

After my sex ed session with Doc, I realized how the barter system almost substituted for God in this place. At the start, I didn't want to get involved with the politics, drugs, or power games. Instead, I played pinochle or gin rummy with Lorraine, June, and Edie one night a week. Other nights, I'd read June's books. And when I could, I ate alone.

One day I walked by the tattooed lady who dished out food. Her tattoos had Nazi swastikas, SS lightning bolts, skulls and crossed bones. She stared at me, then gestured for me to come closer. I bent my head forward to listen, and she whispered in a husky smoker's voice, "I need you to get me some Valium."

I told her to ask someone else. Her eyes turned as flat and gray as the cement floors. I quickly moved ahead in the line. That night, I told June about it.

"That animal is called the Bear," she said. "Never mess with her."

"How did she get the name?" I asked.

"There was a Chinese lady she didn't like. The Bear is part of the Aryan gang. These assholes hate blacks, Jews, Chinese—anyone who's not 'pure' white. But she doesn't mess with me or Edie."

"Why not?"

"Lorraine once told her if she even looks our way with the wrong attitude, she's dead. Bear's a sick fuck, but not a dumb one. She knows Lorraine could snap her in two without even breathing hard."

"What happened to the Chinese lady?"

"One day they found her dead in the shower. She had big claw marks on her cheek. We all knew who did it. Edie came up with the name. She said, 'It was the motherfucking Bear.' The name stuck."

Four days later, I was in line for lunch. The Bear was serving dark brown gravy with little lumps in it like kitty litter. She stopped and held the big serving spoon above my plate, with the gravy dripping on my tray. "I'm scoping you, bitch," she said. "I hear you're tight with the doctor. Get me some fucking Valiums. You give me shit; it won't even be in my hands. See that skinny white babe in the corner? She's the Needle. She's my bunkie. You say no, she feels dissed. It'll be outta my hands."

Instead of thinking strategically, I blurted, "I can't get you any Valiums."

"That's not how it works, nigger-lover. You got three days. You let us down, we'll leave you so close to death, you'll wish you were already there. I never bluff." Then she pulled back the scoop of food and barked, "Next."

I walked to the end of the counter with an empty tray, nervously grabbing at the bread and dessert. The guard named Martha had warned me I'd blow up like a blimp in this place, but I had to eat to survive.

That night, a *Roseanne* rerun was on TV, and the women were laughing. I sat down with Lorraine, June, and Edie to play gin rummy.

"No secrets in this place," Edie said.

"Needle lady's a big problem," June chimed in.

"Wake up, girl," Lorraine said almost fiercely. "You know what we're talking about?"

"Yeah. I'm in trouble because the Nazi broad wants me to get her Valiums." I paused. All three women were studying my face. "But who's this Needle?"

"More of a *what*, really," said June. "But she's dangerous."

"How so?" I asked.

Edie tapped me on my shoulder so I would look at her. "Sicko has different-size sewing needles. Real thin, easy to hide in her hair. She's smooth, pulling a needle out real fast to stab you. She keeps stabbing you, like a million bee stings. She can poke a needle in your eye or throat so quick, you're damaged forever."

Lorraine said, "If the Needle's after you, you got no choice. You must hurt her first. If not, she'll sneak up on you and jam a pin in your ear."

"What if I just get her the Valiums?" I asked.

"Not an option," June said. "Do that and you're their slave.

"The Needle's a twisted motherfucker, no question there," Lorraine added. "But you have to take her seriously!"

My heart thumped a little faster, and I could smell the fear sweat coming out of me. I turned my head away from them to grab a private second as a wave of nausea rumbled through my stomach. Then I had two thoughts: that I hated myself for being a pathetic murderer thrown in with a bunch of lunatics, and that I was terrified.

"Nina girl, you whiter'n toilet paper," Edie said. Then she gently kicked me under the table. June and Lorraine looked at me, looked at each other, and nodded their heads.

"You gonna vomit or shit?" June said, and they all cracked up.

"Look, you're a good Bunkie," June said. "I know you're scared, and you'd better be. But I'm not ready for you to die. We'll help you plan it.

"I have an idea," Edie broke in, "but you better pray for courage—won't work if you go brain dead out of fear. Want to hear it?"

"Yeah," I croaked. My throat felt as if I had just eaten sand.

"Good," said Edie. "First, you need to buy some time." She winked at Lorraine and June. They were all on the same page, plotting my survival.

"How do I do that?"

"Doc's your friend. Tell him you're in trouble. Tell him Needle wants Valium, but you need him to give you crank—whatever's the strongest amphetamines he's got."

"She wants downers—Valium," I said. "Besides, the pills are different size and look way different."

"Doc can fix the size and look," June replied. "Don't worry about that. You need to take her in the opposite direction."

"Get her the drug. She needs Valium to sleep, to shut off her sick mind. Speed will keep her up for a day or two instead—make her crazy, irritable."

"That's some deviant shit, Edie," Lorraine said. "Nice!"

"Then what?" I asked.

"Oh, sweet baby Jesus, wake this lily-white girl up!" June muttered.

"She's new at this," said Edie.

Lorraine poked her finger into my cheek and said, "Here's what to expect. Second day on speed, she be a wreck. You isolate her and break her fingers, smash her head some. Hurt her bad; just don't kill her. That's too much trouble for the whole prison—make you too many enemies. But you've got to hurt her so bad she never gang up with the Bear and fuck with you. Understand me, girl!"

Lorraine spoke with authority and confidence. She was hypnotic. She kept talking to me until my fear began to melt. Edie and June periodically touched calves with me under the table in a sort of primal reassurance that comforted me and reduced my dread. The three of them held me in their net.

Slowly, I began to wake from my fear stupor. I was prey; I was predator; I was animal. A new mix of adrenaline and something very like hope pulsed within me, making me feel alive. I was tasting the elixir of battle. It would be my life or hers. What a clear-cut, unadorned position to be in—them or me. But I had three people wanting to help me, pushing me to be brave and fight, teaching me their ways. In one corner was Nina, the white girl from Milwaukee. In the other corner, a skinny psycho Nazi killer called the Needle. I was in a melodrama that made me laugh and then shudder.

CHAPTER 11

The next time I had Doc alone in his office, I went in and shut the door. "I'm in trouble," I said. "I need your help."

"What's wrong?" he asked.

I told him the situation. He listened patiently, not speaking till I was done.

"I have two pills," he said. "Both strong stimulants that would do the trick. You know, around here we take care of each other." He looked away.

"Doc, I like you, but I just can't have sex with you," I said. "Right now I'm too afraid and my mind is all over the place. If we had sex, it would scramble my mind. I just can't."

"We've been through that," he said. "If you feel obligated to me, then I'll make you a deal. I'll give you the pills. In exchange, when I tell you something private, I want to know you'll keep it to yourself. You already listen to me when I need to talk things over. Now you'll become my official confidante. That can be better than sex."

"You have a deal."

He got up and took a key from his key chain, opened the medicine cabinet, and removed a small bottle from the back. He looked at me with a wicked grin.

"I know the Needle wants Valiums. These pills look similar, but they're something altogether different. They'll have her bouncing off the cot she sleeps on. She'll take one and think something's wrong. Then she'll take the other pill, hoping it'll help her sleep. They'll keep her up for two days and tear up her nerves." He folded the two little white tablets into a square of tissue and handed it to me. "Be careful," he said.

That night after lights-out, June and I went over the plan. I'd give the pills to the Bear tomorrow. The next day, I would attack.

June talked with authority. "Remember, after lunch they both stay in the kitchen, in back. They worked out a deal with the guards so they can run the kitchen. Their Aryan white trash friends work in back with them, too. We have a guard, a big black mama who's our friend. She's going to fetch a few Nazi women out of the kitchen to help clean a huge water spill in the laundry. Edie's arranging the spill. Lorraine bribed the guard. You need to go in back of the kitchen, offering more Valiums to the Needle. You'll be alone with her and the Bear. Neither expects trouble." June paused. "You remember what Lorraine taught you."

My heart was racing again. I was shaking, scared, feeling as I had when we first learned that my brother was shot. The family didn't know his condition, and we waited hours to hear the news. June noticed my trembling body.

"Take a deep breath, honey," she said. "Deep inside. You'll be fine. You have justice on your side. You also have me, Edie, and Lorraine to coach you. We're a fine team. You'll come out of this. Sleep now; there's plenty of time before the action. Save your strength."

A few deep breaths helped calm me. Then a weird thought entered my mind. Other than the junkie who shot my friend Juanita, I had never ever hurt anyone. My appearance was pleasant, but nothing exceptional. Men sometimes commented that my blue eyes were pretty. I had a strong, lean body I was proud of: small breasts like my mother, tall like my dad. But still, just a regular, unspectacular person. Then, in a matter of six months, I had been convicted of murder, and now I was plotting how to seriously hurt two Aryan sadists.

There's something to be said for being in fear for your life. Lying on my cot, locked in, controlling my fear, I could see how ridiculous my life had been. I had been sleepwalking, living with little vitality or passion. If events moved me, I would sway like a branch in the wind. Otherwise, there was little that I cared enough about to get my vital juices up. I had gone through life unaware of how numb I was.

But now I knew I was walking away from my old self. Being locked up and threatened with violence spurred me to wake up. I had the focus of a predator whose life depended on the hunt.

I wondered if Donny had felt like this before jumping out of a helicopter into a foreign desert, ready to kill. Was this what they meant when they said, "You enter war a boy and return a man"? But he went to Desert Storm a boy and returned dead. A corpse is not a man.

Then, with a ripping headache, I thought how Donny would not want me dead. He would kick me the way Edie and June kicked me, so I could wake up and fight the fight—and *live*.

My fear turned into a deep, powerful calm. I was at peace and sure of what had to be done. I would take the Needle and the Bear and punish them. I would bring them pain and hurt them for terrorizing me. They were mine. Why, I wondered, had it taken me so long since Donny's death to want to live?

CHAPTER 12

It was time. This was the Needle's second day of climbing walls on the wrong drugs. We figured she would be wired, scratching at herself, exhausted and drained. And we knew for certain that the Bear would know I had deliberately deceived them.

Cell doors opened for the start of another day. For the first time, the click and bang of all those steel doors opening at the same time didn't put me in a blue funk. Instead of discordant clanging, I heard music. June slapped my ass hard.

"Ouch!" I yelped as my reverie vanished.

"We're with you," she said. "There's no more to say." She smiled down at me, looking gorgeous.

I skipped breakfast. Instead, June brought me food. During the wait, I relaxed. Lorraine had spent time with me alone, teaching me how to fight. She sounded like the coach who keeps yelling for Rocky to hit Apollo Creed in the ribs. It wasn't her words so much as her instinctive attitude and utter lack of qualms about hurting someone. It reminded me of a saying I heard somewhere: *In order to have peace, one must prepare for war.*

I worked alone in the clinic, organizing files. Doc was off in town. People stayed away from me, which, in this perverse environment, amounted to caring. Again I ate alone in my cell.

When lunch was over, I walked into the kitchen, somber and determined to do damage. Summoning clarity, I imagined myself standing in autumn woods, with my breath condensing in the cold, still air. As I entered the harsh gray kitchen, I heard a loud whistle and a commotion coming from the laundry room. Edie was creating a flood. On schedule, Mama Guard came into the kitchen, walked into the back, and marched out with four women.

My heart pounded. So much for temporary calm. Even so, I didn't let my hammering heart distract me, except to notice how thirsty I was. My lips practically stuck together. I licked the roof of my mouth, but it didn't help much. I breathed hard and thought I must resemble a terrorized, amped-up bull about to be ridden in a rodeo.

I walked toward the back. The Needle stood on my right by the huge oven door. She looked at me, and her head moved back and forth in a small, erratic arc. Her eyes, even though wildly dilated, looked weary, with little red worms of broken blood vessels squiggling through the whites. She looked like a pitiful old woman—until she moved. With astonishing speed, she swept her right hand into her hair, and suddenly she held a three-inch sewing needle between thumb and forefinger.

The Bear was by the sink on the opposite side. She looked at me, and a mean grin emerged between her puffy cheeks. "Glad you're here," she said. "You fucked with us. You gave my bunkie speed, you nigger-loving piece of shit. You deliberately gave us the wrong pills."

Ignoring her, I looked at her skinny, wired homegirl. "Here, I have something for you," I said.

The Needle looked at me confused. She kept stretching her head to the side as if she had a kink in her neck. She was pale, thin, wasted. Darting at her, I smashed her in the eye socket with my right fist, then grabbed her hair with the same hand. She pulled back and let out a wild, animal shriek. The noise distracted me. This scrawny creature was quick. She stuck me in the neck with the sewing needle, then ripped downward, slicing through my skin as if it were Jell-O. Pain burned through me as I saw my blood hit the floor.

As I let go of her hair, she raised the needle to eye level, and in that millisecond, I thought I would be blinded. I kicked her hard in the right thigh, and she went down on one knee, wailing.

Knowing that the Bear would be on me any second now, I grabbed a fistful of the Needle's hair and hauled her forward, slamming her nose and chin into the oven door. Palming the back of her head on the rebound, I smashed her into the oven door a second time. She moaned and slumped to the floor. I didn't stop for a second. I wrapped my fingers around her thumb and pulled it back until it broke. Then, grabbing her other hand, I split her index finger away from the others, breaking it. She wouldn't be wielding a needle anytime soon.

Too late, I felt the Bear come up behind me. The punch at the base of my skull filled the air with buzzing black bees. As I staggered away from her, trying to stay on my feet, she came at me again. I thought, *This is it—this is where she kills me.*

My adrenaline was pumping, and a new surge of strength shot through my body just as I felt her thick fingers latch on to my face and squeeze. Those massive fingertips were on my cheekbone, too close to my eyes. Another inch, and they would do what the Needle had failed to do. Unable to break free of those massive hands, I arched backward, but those big, hard fingers kept boring into my face, groping closer to my eyes.

Just as I felt the first fingertip come over the bottom edge of my eye socket, I opened my mouth and counter behind me was a cast-iron skillet. I grabbed it as she charged. How could anyone that size move so fast? Within a second, her fist hit me in the stomach, and I thought I would puke on the spot. She cocked her arm back to hit me again, just as I raised the skillet. She couldn't stop—her fist hit the skillet full force, and I could hear and feel the knuckles turn to red mush. I'll never forget that gut-wrenching moan. With her other hand, she reached for my hair, but I brought the skillet down on her head, and she collapsed to the floor.

I got down on one knee and checked her pulse. Good—it was pumping right along. Next, I laid her right hand out flat and, raising the skillet, smacked it down edgewise on her fingers. She would never again serve me food or claw another woman.

Grabbing a clean, folded dish cloth from a stack on the counter, I pressed it to my bleeding neck. My breath was coming in short, shallow pants. I wondered if I would bleed to death. Deliberately slowing my breath, I walked to the infirmary with both knees wobbling. I tried pretending everything was normal, but in this place such a charade was useless. Everyone knew everything.

Edie came up behind me, put her hand around my shoulder, and walked me into Doc's office. He went to work immediately, getting out a curved needle and sutures and injecting me with an antibiotic and Demerol. The opiate washed through my brain and body like hot soup on a cold day, and my body went into a slight spasm as the tension disappeared. I sat there and wept. Doc put eight stitches in my neck, then gently rubbed antiseptic on the lesion in my cheek. As he was stitching me up, June walked into the room. He looked at her and Edie, then said, "The needle missed her carotid artery by a hair. Even so, she lost a lot of blood. She's lucky it landed in flesh. It was very close."

June wrapped her arm around me and lifted me up to stand. "I got her, Edie," she said. "Thanks, Doc."

June told me to walk with her slow and easy. Standing close to me, she whispered in my ear, "You did good, baby girl. Real good. We gotta get out of here. Doc has a lot of work to do on those two bitches. God *damn*! Needle got you, but you fucked 'em both up for life. I'm real proud, honey. You did good."

We reached our cell. My legs were jelly, and I sagged with exhaustion and the Demerol. I lay down on my cot, and June covered me with a blanket. My eyes refused to stay open. I slept the rest of the day and all night.

When I woke, my first sensation was in my belly. There was a deep purple bruise right above my belly button, and if I breathed with any depth, it felt as if my ribs were breaking. My neck and head throbbed, and the inside of my cheeks felt raw and abraded.

"Take these," June said. "Doc says they'll help with the pain."

I swallowed the two horse pills, then slowly got dressed, and June escorted me to the shower. She waited while I sat on the toilet. I felt like a kid being taken to school on the first day by an overprotective parent. At the same time, her care and concern helped me feel solid again.

Washed and feeling a little better, I said, "Thanks for everything."

"We're real proud of you, Nina. You've been through the storm. Now it's important for you to eat. Let's go."

We walked to the kitchen, and June stood behind me in line. When we reached the woman serving the food, she looked at me with a smile and put two portions of eggs on my plate. They were delicious.

CHAPTER 13

After the fight, life returned to a monotonous routine, which I didn't mind. I found out that prison had a rigid protocol, an unspoken code. The Bear and the Needle were so beaten that their allies refused to help them. They had brought shame on the Aryan group by having a single, scrawny white girl take them on at the same time and kick their asses. More important, I earned a degree of respect from the other inmates. This reduced my fear some but did nothing to relieve the low-grade depression. The isolation combined with the violence and the unrelenting gray of my surroundings left me despondent. I was a robot again, not human. Empty inside.

I was in the yard before my work shift. The yard is about the size of a high school football field. I went off into a corner section, where no other inmates were standing around. In my pants pocket was an unopened letter from Steven—my first letter since being inside.

Steven and I had been writing off and on for years. The anguish we felt at losing Donny had changed us both in a profound way. Somehow, we shared a spiritual intimacy, because Donny was the person we both loved. Steven wasn't afraid to cry and express his grief for Donny with the same abandon I did. We avoided discussions about the past, but I could tell that he still hurt from losing his dearest friend.

It felt like having a pen pal living in a different country. I flew to Wyoming for his wedding to a schoolteacher named Linda. About two years after their wedding, they had a baby girl they named Lydia.

Steven ran the family ranch thirty miles outside Jackson Hole, Wyoming. In the summer, he guided fly fishermen on the Snake, Green, New Fork, and Salt rivers. He had fished Wyoming's rivers all his life, and now he earned money doing something he loved. During the winter, he did well as an advertising photographer, doing nature and animal shots for ads. He once explained to me that he would showcase a product, featuring friends with faces weathered by the outdoors. He told me that a large bank used a lot of his shots in its billboard ads, preferring his style because it had "real people." For his clients, he still shot photos with a film camera. He was adept at using digital, but he liked the old-fashioned grain from film stock.

Time moved quickly, and we didn't write for a couple of years except for the occasional postcard when either of us went somewhere on vacation. About a year before I went up, Steven started to write me long letters. The tone changed, and he included complex feelings about his life. His letters moved me, and I wrote back. I didn't know how to write about my most intimate feelings—most of the time I didn't even know what they were. But I could express how much I understood and cared about him.

When my case exploded and I needed help, Steven flew to San Francisco. He met the lawyer and watched the wheeling and dealing, and he took me out and tried to cheer me up. He offered support and money. I didn't want money, but I needed him to reassure my mom and dad, to ease their fear and worry. I loved my parents deeply, and I was sad and ashamed for bringing such stress into their life. For them, my going to prison was as if I were being exiled to some remote jungle.

Once I was officially convicted and about to serve time, Steven closed down my apartment for me, shipping my few valuables to his ranch. He sold my stereo, TV, and furniture and put the money in an account for me. He called my parents and assured them that I would be out of prison in a few years. They wanted to visit, but I pleaded with them not to travel to California to see me in prison. I promised I would call and write them. The only reason they complied was my mother's failing health. At the same time, Steven tried to assuage their fear and promised he would visit and look after me.

The night before I was to surrender to the authorities, Steven told me how bad things were between Linda and him. They didn't fight and they didn't make love. They hung out in some god-awful limbo, like the stereotypical old married couple in a restaurant who never look at each other and swallow their food in silence.

I wrote him about the fight with the two Aryan sickos. Several weeks later, I received his long letter.

Dear Nina,

I'm so proud of the way you kicked ass. Your friends remind me of Larry, Donny, and me getting ready for battle. You walk into the fight realizing you might not return. I bet you felt empty of thoughts, and exhilarated in a strange way. Often a fight lacks forgiveness; you're going to get hurt or hurt somebody else. It changes your heart when you decide to risk everything and face your enemies. Especially when you come out in one piece.

I'm proud because you displayed great courage walking into that kitchen like a frightened but focused warrior. I have to ask, while you were on the way to the kitchen, did you pee in your pants?

When I grew up in Jackson Hole, my friends and I were dudes, real dudes, fishing and hunting, riding horses, shooting guns. We wore cowboy boots, smoked, and talked the big talk. I had an Indian friend who taught me how to wrestle and how to sweat with his uncles in the lodge. I had a code of behavior: loyalty, being a gentleman, fighting when I had to, being there for family and friends. To some people I sound prudish. I took great pride in the fact that we were rugged. Part of that was exaggerated, egotistical, and a little macho, yet a bunch of my kid values were real and healthy.

Now when I walk around Jackson Hole, I see yuppies with cell phones and very expensive cowboy boots that have never stepped anywhere near a cow pie. They drive high-end SUVs but can't camp out alone in the woods. They fly-fish with expensive equipment. I still tie my own flies and use an old bamboo rod. I also see a lot of angry older kids with big, bad attitudes. Often there's very little backbone behind it. Okay, let's have a rousing yawn for my commentary on the changing times. What I really want to tell you is this:

You already know my relationship with Linda has been crap for some time. I didn't ever contemplate walking away, and in some remote fantasy universe, I had hoped we could put it together again. I wanted it to work. Well, last month I found out Linda's been having an affair with some computer guy who works at the new software company outside of town. Me, the old dude, and there's a techno-nerd yuppie having sex with my wife.

At first I wanted to hurt him. I also felt my self-image as a man wilt like a balloon losing air. So I went to his apartment and picked him up off the ground—almost gave myself a hernia. Then he said, "Hey, man, she wanted this affair." Strange, but when I realized he wasn't to blame, my blind fury subsided. Then I told him, "I don't care if she was dancing naked while screaming for you to devour her. You had something to do with breaking us up. You're a moral punk." Then I gave him a light punch in the ribs just so he'd know I had been there. Don't worry, I didn't break anything. Now that you're kind of a bad-ass, do you think I should have induced just a little pain?

When I got back home, Linda and I fought for an hour. I wanted to scream, and I had this silly image of pouring cold beer over her head. I calmed down and told her how her betrayal hurt me. She told me I had been emotionally distant for far too long. We blamed each other until we ran out of words. Then we sat and stared at each other for an uncomfortable couple of minutes. Finally, I said what we both clearly recognized: "It's over." She nodded and began to cry.

I didn't feel the least shred of sadness. It's hard to explain. It was like taking a roll of film and capturing pictures I cared about. Then suddenly, someone opens the camera in the daylight, and the film is exposed and ruined. Our marriage was like that exposed roll of film—fifteen years, all useless and ruined.

I felt sick at my stomach; then the nausea vanished. I told her, "I don't care how frustrated you were—I didn't deserve betrayal." She asked me not to hate her, explaining in three very simple sentences what happened. "I felt cut off from you. I met him and fell in love. I'm sorry it happened this way." Nina, why is life so easy to explain for some people? Three lousy sentences and she said it all. Piss on succinctness.

Meanwhile, our prodigy daughter, fifteen going on thirty-five, heard the content of the fight. She had already known because one of her girlfriends—I think the one who wears lime-green nail polish and a ring in one nostril, told Lydia she saw her mom with some guy in an espresso shop. They were holding hands and laughing. So Lydia knew her mom was having an affair. She also knew I'd be hurt. She's very protective of me. Once she overheard our fight, I think she felt relief because she didn't have to hold the secret any longer.

Anyway, once everything was out in the open, I went from anger and frustration to hopelessness. I just wanted to get away. I told Linda I needed an hour to think things over and was going to take a walk. She welcomed the break. I walked on an old trail that passes through a grove of lodgepole and meanders over a stream. Spring was breaking early this year, and it was unusually warm. Birds and cicadas were singing their songs. I splashed in the stream, scaring a little water snake. As I stepped out of the water, I had a very simple realization: If she wants this guy, he can have her. I want her out of my life as soon as possible.

We met back in the living room and started talking. I felt calm, but it wasn't a healthy calm. It was more like going to a funeral without being able to feel the loss of the dead person, because you just don't care.

I told her to pack and be out of the house in a week. At first, she wanted more time. So I asked her to be packed and out in two weeks. She started to object, and I said, "You are fucking another man and are still married to me. As long as you lie naked and take him into your body and heart, I don't ever want to share a bathroom, kitchen, or shelter with you. Don't argue and try to stay in our home. This is my house and it was my grandfather's house, so we're not splitting it. I want you out, and this discussion is over." She nodded and said okay.

I told her I would leave during the packing up and dismantling of our marriage. I also told her Mr. Computer Chip was not allowed on the property to help her move. Then I took out our checkbooks and savings passbook to figure out what we had: not that much, not that little. I wrote her a check for over half of what we had in checking, and gave her most of the savings. I figured that was fair and honorable. Then I thought, fuck her—get out of here. The emotional good-bye reminded me of when they cut my hair in the army. I was nearly bald and felt naked. Strange image to have after fifteen years of marriage goes down the drain.

"What about Lydia?" she asked me.

I said, " Lydia wants to live with me while you adventure

into a new life. You will always be her mother, and I'll never interfere with that. I'll pay for college when she goes. You can see her, help her, love her any way you want. She can stay at your new place as much as she wants. I'll never talk bad about you to her. That's a promise."

June walked over to me in the southwest corner of the yard and looked at my face.

"What's up, sunshine?" she asked.

"A letter from a good friend. He was with my brother, Donny, in Kuwait and Iraq.

"You feeling okay?"

"Yeah. I'm coming back to myself. Thanks. You're a terrific friend."

"No big deal. You're either a friend or a taker. Hey, you're in a serious mood, I can tell. Everything okay with this man?"

"Not really. I'll tell you later," I said.

"Okay, then. Remember, cards tonight. It'll be our first game since the big ass-whup. I know Edie and Lorraine will enjoy a worry-free night."

"Me, too," I said as June walked across the yard. It seems a little bizarre in retrospect, but I found myself thinking how lucky I was to have such a gem for a cellmate.

I was alone again. The letter was burning in my pants pocket. I couldn't wait to get back to it. I had fifteen minutes of free time left. I turned my body away from the center of the yard and faced the wall. It was as much privacy as I could grab in this terrarium. I opened the letter and began where I had left off:

After the confrontation and my request (or ultimatum, depending on how you look at it) that she pack and leave, I went into the mountains to see my old friend and teacher, Eagle Heart. When I was young, Eagle Heart took a liking to me. He loves to fish, so one year I made him some special flies as a gift. Years later, he spent time tuning me for the war. He told me what it takes to be a warrior. More than anything, he believed in me as a man. He has great affection for me, and most important, he's the only truly wise person I know in my life.

When I got to his house on the reservation, he looked me up and down and said, "Your woman found another man. Come, we'll go to the sweat lodge and talk after."

The lodge is round and made of canvas held up by carved bark, with a couch-size pit in the middle. The men chant and pray. The younger men use pitchforks to bring in red-hot rocks that have been sitting in a huge fire for several hours, and put them in the pit. Then water is poured on them, and the lodge gets really hot.

My first few sweats, I thought I would melt. But as time went on, I found the drum and the chanting had a meditative effect a lot like fly-fishing. I got out of my mind and thoughts. The difference, I suppose, is that the sweat ritual is directed towards healing. They say it brings you closer to the Great Spirit.

Eagle Heart brought in a large round drum for chanting. I had to throw tobacco into a fire outside the lodge, symbolizing my asking the Great Spirit for guidance. Once we were inside and the ritual began, Eagle Heart ordered his nephew to close the flap. It was as dark as a moonless night without stars. In the pit, the hot rocks gave off an eerie glow. Eagle Heart hit the drum while his nephew poured more water on the rocks. They sizzled, and the searing heat hit my skin. Eagle Heart immediately instructed me to chant with him. The drum became hypnotic, and I stopped thinking about my wife or the heat. My body reacted to the steam, and sweat poured off me. I felt totally enveloped in the heat and the comfort of being with Eagle Heart. Suddenly, I felt an explosion deep inside me. Then I began to cry. I hadn't cried since Donny's death. As I cried, the drumming grew louder. Although there were other men in the sweat, I felt alone and respected. Then, as abruptly as it began, the emotion stopped, and at that split second, Eagle Heart opened the canvas flap.

Fresh air filtered in with the light. He gestured to me to leave and walked me to the river. We both jumped in. He said, "Wash away the pain."

The cold river shocked me into feeling utterly alive. Next, Eagle Heart wrapped a woven blanket around me and cloaked himself in another. We walked into a meadow, where he instructed me to face east and talk to the spirits. He told me to ask for Linda to be protected and to ask the Great Mystery to absorb my rage and hurt. After I did this, he told me to face north and ask the Great Spirit for self-forgiveness. Next, I faced west and asked for the ability to love again. I faced every direction with a different prayer, until I felt a peaceful stillness come over me. When I finished, we got dressed and went to his home, where his large family was preparing a huge dinner. Everyone laughed and treated me as an honored guest.

It's been a few months since that experience. Now that Linda is living with her boyfriend, I've been spending more time with Lydia. She's real smart, but she hangs out with some stupid, angry punk kids. Last week I took her into the mountains to fish and horseback ride. She drilled me about my broken marriage. "Dad, I don't want you to be lonely," she said. She was really sweet. I told her the truth: her mother had made it easy for me to let go.

This letter is going on longer then I intended. Don't let prison life get you down. Time flies when you're in love and moves slow as cold molasses when you're locked up. Regardless, you'll be out soon.

Steven

Folding Steven's letter, I felt a sudden clarity, as if I were in an airplane and my ears popped. His life and the vivid descriptions were like a gift: they brought me hope. I wasn't sure what to be hopeful about, but the letter counterbalanced my sense of dread, giving my floundering spirit a little jump start.

CHAPTER 14

That night, June and I talked for about twenty minutes until she fell asleep. Once again I lay on my back, looking up at June's mattress springs as they dissolved into a blank palette for my vivid imagination. What came out of my unconscious was a storybook review of men. Men—not my arena of greatest success in life.

At first, I thought that Steven's letter was waking a long-dormant part of my womanhood: desire. The idea vanished like the cloud formations in a mountain thunderstorm. I suddenly saw myself when I was twenty-six, seriously dating this guy I had met in the office cafeteria where we both worked.

Lenny and I first dated by going to movies, having dinner, and taking walks. It was slow and relaxed, and he seemed a really nice guy. We talked on the phone but avoided contact at work. Fortunately, he worked in the next building, so it wasn't a problem. I hadn't been with a man in two years. I wasn't a virgin, but close to it. Not that I didn't want sex—I just couldn't get naked and make love when my feelings about some guy were mixed with indifference. I had no moral judgments toward girlfriends who loved to talk about sex. I wasn't saving it for marriage. Rather, I was saving it for some inner comfort and ease that I hadn't yet experienced. So the few times I had sex, it wasn't much fun, profound, or memorable.

One time Lenny took me out to a nice restaurant, and afterward we went back to his apartment. He poured some wine, put his arm around me, bent down to kiss me, and began the whole intimacy ritual. I decided to give it a try.

After about fifteen minutes of kissing and feeling my breasts, Lenny began groping me. I was high from the wine, and we both got undressed. I remember how skinny he looked, almost funny with his erection standing out as if to offer a salute. He got on top of me and tried, with a complete lack of grace, to put it in me. As much as I wanted there to be some beauty and tenderness in our lovemaking, he reminded me of a grunting, salivating ape, lacking any erotic appeal whatever. I grabbed him and put him inside me, and he pumped away until he came, then climbed off me and went into the bathroom. Right there, I decided to end our relationship. I got up, put on my clothes, and left. At home, I called him and told him it wasn't going to work. We didn't have a prayer of success, and I wished him well.

June suddenly turned over in her bunk, and the mattress springs made a metallic creaking sound. The train of Lenny images disappeared—that memory was over for now. Men—I couldn't stop thinking about men. Steven had a core of decency combined with a tough male resilience that was new for me. In his letter, he had talked to me with an honesty that penetrated my jailhouse lethargy.

Sometimes the women moved around and visited one another during meals. Since Edie and June were almost always around, I didn't usually get to be alone with Lorraine, but the next morning we had breakfast together. Lorraine was different today, so strong and sweet. I relished the idea of just the two of us talking.

"What's on your mind, sweetie?" she asked.

"Men," I said. "Last night I couldn't stop thinking about all my shitty relationships."

"Men can be poison through and through, or they can soothe you inside and out." She laughed at her silly joke. I laughed with her.

"I have a simple belief about men," she said.

"What's that?" I asked.

"Most of 'em really suck. It's not that they think with their dick—everyone knows that, but that's not what bothers me. In fact, sometimes I like that. What pisses me off is how fuckin' blind they can be. Their hearts are covered with ice."

"I think I know a man who's really different." I said.

"Tell me in a minute. I didn't finish. I believe, in our lifetime, there's one man, maybe just one, who is different. Who is really kind and loving. I think every woman has a hard-assed journey going through men until she meets that one guy who deserves her love. A lot of women never find him, because they get bitter after a while. But that one guy is out there. Look at June. Her hubby's a good man. Not perfect, but a good man."

"How'd you get so wise?" I said, and hugged her.

"Be careful with that hugging stuff in here, sweetie. Old Lorraine has enemies. But I think I know the answer to your question." She stared off into space, milking the moment until I would say something.

"What's that," I asked."

"Simple, sweetie," Lorraine chuckled. "God looked at me and said, 'I love you, but *damn*, you sure are ugly. I need something to balance things out. How 'bout I give this woman a dose of wisdom? This way, you look at her face and hear her wisdom, and you realize her worthiness." Lorraine stopped and acted as though she was trying to recall something profound.

I grinned. "Yeah, tell me, Lorraine. What did God say?"

"Well, God came up with a very amazing saying that was on account of me. He said, "People will look at her and discover, *beauty is only skin deep*." Then God cracked up and said, "'Cause she sure is ugly, and now she sure is wise."' Lorraine cackled so loud, I thought one of the guards would come over and tell us to shut up.

"Now, tell me, sweetie, you ever marry?" Lorraine asked.

"I married a guy when I was twenty-six. He was a nice guy, and we had some good times together," I said. "But in a strange way, I don't remember much. There was no abuse, and there was no deep love. I divorced him. I had little feeling about it. Afterwards, it was strange, like moving to another city and knowing you won't see a friend anymore, but also knowing that's okay."

"Why you never feel love for a man?" she asked.

"I never thought about it until I landed in this pit," I said.

"Well, sometimes we have nothing left to do but think. You know why?"

"Something happened to me when my brother got killed," I said. "Something inside me turned off. Know what I mean?"

"I know something but don't have the words for it. I can only feel it."

"Try. Just try and tell me," I said.

Lorraine frowned for a moment, organizing her thoughts. "Maybe you don't think you deserve love, because your brother got killed. I can't explain it, but you live like you're holding back, waiting. When you lost your brother, you lost a piece of yourself. I can't explain it better than that."

I said, "The letter I got from Steven has shaken me up some."

"Prison isolates us," she said. "Maybe this is your time to prepare for that one man in your life. Remember my words. Us women look for that one man. It could take a lifetime to find him, but all we want is that one special man. Got to believe he's out there. Everyone else is just noise."

CHAPTER 15

It was April, and the rainy season was over. The air was clean. Spring in this part of California was far less dramatic than in Milwaukee, where you moved from a freezing chill to balmy warmth. Here it was always mild.

One day, two things happened that gave me some direction and purpose. First, I was called in to see the warden. After my battle with the Bear and the Needle, I thought surely I would be summoned by her and punished for fighting, yet nothing had happened.

"Please sit down," she said. "You may call me Warden."

I sat in a cheap leather chair. She was in a high-backed chair behind a heavy antique oak desk. Her office was paneled with dark mahogany. One wall had a long bookshelf of hardcover books. The books looked like props on a movie set.

The warden was in her mid-fifties and slender. She wore her hair short and had round tortoiseshell glasses. Above her lip was a mole with a little tuft of hairs growing out of it. I wondered why she didn't pluck them with tweezers or have them removed with electrolysis.

"What do you miss most?" she asked.

I hesitated, suspecting a trick. "I miss colors," I finally said. "I am sick to death of dreary gray. I'd like some blues and yellows. Not loud and bright—just a little color to make me feel better." I looked away, feeling that it wasn't safe to talk honestly with her. She seemed to sense my sudden apprehension.

"We have a few things to talk about," she said. "You're a short-timer. You get out in about a year." She paused. When she continued, her tone sounded more rigid and rehearsed. "Do not for one minute think I wasn't aware of what happened in the kitchen. I see the scar on your neck, and I know all about your confrontation. I could have called you in and tagged on another year for fighting."

"Thank you for not—"

She cut me off. "I didn't bust your ass, for a reason—because you served a purpose. Remember that."

"What was that, Warden?"

"Have you ever gone to the circus?"

"Yes," I said. What a question. Was she toying with me?

"In the circus there are many elephants."

I looked at her and nodded. "Yes, many elephants. Big elephants."

Her eyes narrowed. Her jaw moved as if she was raking her teeth back and forth. I realized she was angry. "Don't be glib with me—I don't appreciate sarcasm."

"I won't, Warden."

She lightened up as if she had undergone a very fast mood swing. "In the circus, there's a man who goes behind the elephants with a big shovel. Every time an elephant shits, he scoops it up."

"Quite a job," I said.

"In your fight with the lovely Aryan scum, you became the guy picking up the elephant shit. You helped clean the circus arena for me. That's why you weren't called in."

"I never looked at it that way," I said.

"Let me enlighten you about what really goes on here," she said. "We have some sick and nasty women in this place. All they know—and want to know—is pain and degradation. Some of these animals will never change. They were born, and will die, knowing only hatred. The two women you permanently maimed have decided to become passive in this hole. Do you know why?"

"No, Warden."

"Because they were broken. Once you brought them down, their Aryan sisters deserted them. Are you listening?"

"Yes, Warden."

"Weakness doesn't exist long in this place. Weakness brings shame to their gang."

"I didn't know that. Why are you telling me this?" I asked.

Her face went through another angry contortion. "Because I want to," she snapped. "Never ask me *why* I am doing something!"

I realized that the warden needed to control people but that, deep down, she didn't have the confidence to be a boss. There was a false ring somewhere in that hard-assed persona. Yet I knew that in the prison world, I was her slave and she was my master. To pretend otherwise would only hurt me.

She went on. "You could take most of these inmates and offer them a private meeting with Jesus, and afterwards, they would go right back out and steal, kill, shoot up, or hurt someone. I think some of these people belong in the zoo, which is another name for our psychiatric clinic. Their brains are missing a switch that turns on a very important lightbulb. They don't have any sense of right and wrong and never will."

"Warden, may I ask you a question?" I said, careful to emanate all the humility I could.

"What?"

"Do you see everyone as hopeless?"

"I play the numbers as if it were a horse race. At least half the women in for hard time will fuck up outside. Once they're caught, they return. We have a rotating door for half our population. The younger ones are the worst. About sixty percent return within two years. Some women in here can't make it on the outside—they lack the job skills and motivation."

"Can you help them?" I asked.

"I'm not a guidance counselor. Politically, the population on the outside wants to see criminals punished, not educated. Dollars rule this animal house. Look at the last governor. What a moron—he had less common sense than some of my inmates!" She stopped talking and looked at me in an odd way. "Listen carefully," she said. "There are some women in here who have potential. They made mistakes and are paying for them. I don't want them back. Right now we have about ten women leaving this prison within the next nine to twelve months. Your bunkie, June, is one of them. If they get outside and only speak their ethnic slang, only Spanglish or homey bullshit, they won't get a job."

"So?" I asked.

"So! I want you to teach them to speak English in complete sentences. I want you to get them prepared for job interviews, get them speaking business English so they can get a job. I want them to keep their jailhouse rap out of the workplace. Most important, I want them to succeed. For me, political correctness has as much value as a used tampon. Understand me?"

"Yes, I understand—"

She held up her hand. "Stop right there. I'm going to save you from the consequences of the 'Why?' you were just about to ask me. Two reasons: I'm sick of seeing them return and live on the state's dime. I don't like running a welfare house. When I keep someone from returning, it's a feather in my cap. That feather can land me a job in Sacramento, managing prison work and far away from this slime."

"But . . . why me?"

"It says in your file you went to college and were an English major. We have no money for an outside teacher. The governor thinks it's a luxury expense. You're the one. I'm going to give you a list of ten women. Just tell me what you'll need to teach them business English."

"But I'm not a teacher," I said.

"You are now. What will you need to make this work?"

I hesitated and looked down to my left. I looked back up at the warden and then down again. I knew there was no talking my way out of this. She was the boss, and she had made her decision to use me as a guidance counselor before I walked into this room. Why was a moot question. So I took the question and seriously pondered my new job. I looked her in the face, not feeling frightened or passive.

"A meeting room, paper, and pencils."

"You'll do well to remember a couple of things," she said. "You owe me. I never busted you for fighting. This is payback time. That means I expect you to work hard at this."

"Okay," I said.

"Just focus on how you can help them get jobs by speaking good English. It offers them a chance to make it on the outside."

"Anything else I should know?" I asked.

"Yeah. Avoid politics. No whining and blaming the system. Don't treat them like victims. Fuck how hard life has been. Jobs go to people who can speak well and make a decent presentation. Go for reality; the rest is bullshit." She got up, opened the door, and ushered me out.

Just as I was walking away, she said, "And, Nina, I'm going to get blue paint for the infirmary. I don't need you so damn melancholy." Then she closed the door.

That night, I told June about my meeting with the warden. She listened and then spoke with slow and perfect diction. "Hello, my name is June. May I go to the bathroom before we discuss how to market toilet paper?" She laughed at her words. "Nice, round bullshit whitebread speech. No colloquialism on the job."

"There's no choice here, babe."

"How you say it long?" she asked.

"There is no other option available right now."

"Fuck me—you're a teacher!" She laughed as she said it.

I knew that June could speak like a ghetto black or a college professor. There were many sides to this woman. Some people got real hungry for chat intimacy here in prison. June had no need for me to get to know her intimately, and that transformed our relationship into mutual respect and friendship and allowed us to understand each other quickly.

Then I remembered something that had been bothering me. Lorraine seemed depressed and anxious. Her tough veneer and usual good humor had evaporated. The last time Edie, Lorraine, June, and I had played cards, Lorraine was morose. Something was going on, but no one offered me an explanation. So I decided to talk it over with June.

"What's with Lorraine?" I said. "She looks worried."

"She's in trouble with the Rose. She stole some drugs off their dumb mule. Mexican gang is big here. I get along with them. I stay away. This time, Lorraine has to fix it. It's not an easy situation."

"Can I help? What's this about the Rose?"

"No, you'd just get yourself killed by the Rose. She's their leader. Lorraine broke the big rule. She must fix it. It can't be our fight. We'll stand by her, but she needs to fix it. Mexican gang is very pissed. The Rose lives for this conflict. She feeds on violence and tension like a baby sucking mother's milk."

I asked again, "Can't I?"

"Don't even think about it. You can't undo this. Now, I need some sleep. We'll talk tomorrow. G'night."

CHAPTER 16

The next day, Doc called me into his office and shut the door. He looked pale, with dark bags under his eyes. I wasn't sure why, but I knew he hadn't traded sex for drugs in at least two months. During that time, we had several long conversations. He told me about growing up poor in a little coal town. When he was seventeen, he won a scholarship to Kentucky State. He worked his way through medical school. After his wife died of breast cancer, he decided never to remarry, because he didn't want to lose anyone again. I thought about my brother. When someone we love dies, we sometimes make decisions that aren't the healthiest.

Doc came to the prison on Monday, Wednesday, and Friday. Usually, when he treated the women around here, he was always ready with a joke. Lately, though, his humor had vanished. I didn't feel it was my business to ask him what was up. As it turned out, I didn't need to ask. He began our conversation in a raspy voice. I thought I saw sadness in his eyes.

"Nina, I know you feel something is wrong," he said.

"You're not yourself, Doc. Can I help?"

"I don't know—got a cure for cancer up your sleeve?"

"How bad is it?"

"There's a small lump in my liver. They'll remove it in two days. Then I have to continue with chemotherapy."

"Have you been on chemo for some time?"

"Yes. A pathetic, debilitating way to live. It can kill the cancer, but it also kills you. For instance, I can't even get an erection." Then he laughed and said, "Not even if it was for you."

I smiled and held his hand. "Doc, if it would help, I'd make love to you in a heartbeat."

"You're sweet," he said. "I might make use of that offer in my fantasy world. Right now my penis has turned to rubber. Can you believe my two favorite indulgences have gone the way of a migrating bird? I can't keep food down, and I have no sexual capacity. What a setup this old man used to have. I shouldn't complain."

"How serious is the cancer?" I said.

"When they remove it, if it hasn't spread, I'll live. I'll be weak and miserable from the chemo, but I'll live. If they find one fingernail's worth of cancer spreading through my body, I figure I have six months to two years left on this earth."

"I'm so sorry," I said. "You've been very kind to me."

"I like you, Nina. You're not hard, yet you're not soft. If you can keep your ground, your center of gravity, in this place, you'll build something good in your life again."

I reached over and held him. He shook in my arms. Before anything could be said, we heard a commotion outside the door.

The nurse screamed, "Doc, hurry!"

We ran into the treatment room. On the metal table was a woman burned beyond recognition. I instinctively knew it was Lorraine. A friend standing beside her was shaking visibly. She said, "The Mexican gang poured boiling water over her head and face."

I couldn't stop staring at her blistered skin. One eye seemed melted. She had gone into cardiac arrest.

"Quick, bring me a syringe of epinephrine!" Doc yelled in a clear voice. As soon as the nurse brought the prefilled syringe, he stabbed it into Lorraine's heart and injected it. Nothing. Next he hit her with electrical stimulation to jolt her back to life. Still no response. She lay on the table like a big, black fish not wanting to go back to sea. It was over. Looking down at her, I saw the scars on her face and hands that mapped out her life. Her burns were grotesque. I covered her with a blanket and stared at her lifeless body.

I remembered the talk we had as she prepared me for my fight. She said she had bounced out of the womb into a drug-crazed household and began fighting for her life from day one. By the time she was six, she was taking care of three children younger than she. Her father left home, and her mother was drunk or stoned most of the time. Lorraine grew up tough and hard, but she could love and care for a select few. She was loyal to her friends.

I wondered how she could end up disfigured and dead in a prison system where she knew the rules better than anyone. For her to steal drugs from the Mexicans was more than a stupid mistake—it was a death wish. Everything she did was deliberate.

Lorraine had taught me with abandon how to fight for myself. When she played cards, she laughed and never complained about what a truly miserable hand life had dealt her. Then I remembered her humor: *"God said, 'She sure is ugly, and now she sure is wise."* That must be where the cliché comes from—beauty is only skin deep. Amen, Lorraine, amen.

I couldn't stand it. Lorraine was gone. I would never see her again. The vapor of her death was swirling all around me. For one brief flash, I saw my brother Donny. Then I remembered a little poem he wrote in a letter from Desert Storm. We got it a week before he was killed.

> *Death is all around;*
> *there's nothing I can do.*
> *Life is leaving my friends*
> *till they find someplace new.*

That night at supper, I walked into the dining room and headed back to where the Mexican gang hung out, eating and talking. All the women were laughing. Their leader, the Rose, was beautiful and ugly at the same time. Her hair and eyes were black. She was about five feet six and muscular, with big, firm breasts, and she stood straight as a board, her head hung back a few degrees to give off an air of arrogance like one of those idiot wrestlers on TV. With a permanent sneer as if her upper lip were welded to her gums, she looked like an attack dog. She seemed to enjoy her cruelty.

She watched me approach to within arm's reach.

"You killed my friend," I said in a surprisingly calm voice. Then I slapped her across the face.

She grabbed my arm and twisted me around as if I were a rag doll, then put her arm under my head and pushed me away. I landed on my hip about three feet from her. She walked over. Everyone in the dining room was mesmerized.

"This time I let you hit me," she said. "You're loyal to your nigger friend. I can respect that. Don't ever touch me again or I'll kill you. Your friend should never have stole from me. She knew that. Now get the fuck outta here!"

I got up, looked her in the face, and walked away.

The room was a blur. I couldn't focus on any faces. I walked out and returned to my cell. June and Edie were in the hallway outside the door of the cell. June looked at me and started to say something. But before a word could come out, she choked up and started crying. Edie and I joined her until all our tears were cried out.

CHAPTER 17

Three days after the Rose and her homies killed Lorraine, Martha came to my cell just before breakfast.

"Eat fast," she said. "You got a visitor."

I was shocked. I thought I had arranged things so no one would visit me.

I ate, and she took me to a room that looked like a high school cafeteria, with long tables and hard metal chairs. They let people walk around instead of sitting opposite each other. I had always pictured thick glass partitions, where convict and visitor talked over a phone while looking and feeling pathetically remote from each other. Some movies had them touching the glass in the same place, as if transmitting some invisible emotional bond. I guessed maybe that setup was for maximum-security prisons, because this room was very different—full of energetic little kids yelling and playing with their moms.

In walked Steven, and I felt my heart do a little skip.

I was struck by how good he looked. His body was lean and strong, and he was dressed in black jeans and an old green flannel shirt. His blue eyes seemed sad. He walked over and stopped a few feet in front of me, and I felt self-conscious. He smiled as if to tell me to relax.

"Hi, Nina," he said, and handed me a book.

I wanted to hug him. He must have known, because he reached

out his long arms and wrapped them around my shoulders. Lowering his hands on my back, he pulled me close. It wasn't sexual exactly—more a sensation of joyous abandon rushing through my body. I pulled away, and he laughed.

"That feels good," he said, with a sort of goofy grin on his face. "They did a very thorough strip search, by the way. If I'd wanted to sneak you in so much as a candy bar, they would have found it."

"Doesn't matter," I replied as I felt some semblance of composure return. "This is amazing! You visiting me . . . here. Why'd you come?" My entire existence in this drab, miserable cave revolved around women. Hell, besides Doc, here was the first man I'd spoken to in over a year and a half. I couldn't stop my emotions from bouncing around like fireflies on a hot summer night. Finally I just grinned.

"You okay?" he asked.

"Sometimes. Without my roommate, June, and a few friends, I'd be either dead or sweating from fear every second. You never know who'll turn on you. Most of the time, I think I'm too soft for this place, but I've come a long way."

There was still that sad look in his eyes. "When you wrote me about fighting those two women who wanted to hurt you, I wondered if that gave you confidence."

"Yeah, it did, in a sick kind of way. It showed me that I enjoyed bringing pain to two sickos. So what does that make me?"

He looked pensive for a moment. "Realistic," he said. "You're drawing on a strong instinct to survive. You can be proud of that, not ashamed. When your brother and I were out there fighting in the desert, it wasn't that we felt relief or joy in killing or inflicting pain on the enemy. What I mean is, there *was* a kind of pleasure in knowing we had survived another fight—in knowing that it was them and not us."

I needed to think about that, so I changed the topic. I looked down at the book he had brought me: *Last of the Breed*, by Louis L'Amour.

"It's one of my favorite survival stories." He laughed. "Not exactly a book about finding your higher self, but I figured a good action story would take your mind away."

"What's it about?" I asked, picturing cowboys shooting it out at a dead run on horseback.

"A Navy pilot is shot down in Russia during the Cold War. He's a Native American with an uncanny ability to outfox his enemy. His goal isn't just to make it through the harsh winter while crossing Russia alone and on foot, but to cross the sea into Alaska. He outwits the Soviet army and Siberian tribespeople."

"You trying to tell me I'm a duck out of water?" I teased.

"Nina, you are a *goldfish* out of water. I bet you never even stole bubble gum, and here you are with killers, sadists, and small-time lowlifes who've spent too much time at both ends of the brutality equation. The point of the book is pure escape. I love the guy's writing."

I stiffened. "There are some fine women in this place. My roommate's very special. You know I . . ."

Steven watched me pause and seemed to understand that his visit had brought me a strange discomfort. He shifted the conversation.

"I had time off from my job," he said. "I wanted to fly down from Wyoming and let you know you have a friend. I wish I lived a little closer and could come here more often."

"Thanks."

We sat quietly for a while. I looked over at the next table, where a little girl was sitting down. She had these beautiful dark braids, and her mother was stroking her face. The husband was gentle looking. I wondered if she was in for long. It must be hell on a kid.

"Your letter meant a lot to me," I said. "How's Lydia?"

His whole face lit up. "My girl's sixteen and growing up fast. I really hate what's going on in the schools—all the drugs and sex. So I'm probably overprotective. Linda's living with the guy I wrote you about, and doesn't want to be a full-time mother. So Dad here gets the job. It's fine by me. I have Lydia's friends over, and some of them play with their hair at the dinner table. Some of 'em are uninhibited slobs, which kind of surprises me. I think their parents must be in another zone, or maybe I'm just old-fashioned and out of touch. Old-fashioned manners, that's me."

"It's the age," I said. "I bet your girl has manners."

"You're right. I have to give Linda credit for that—she taught Lydia good manners."

We both looked around. It was heart-melting to see these women being so tender with their families.

Steven turned back to me and said, "Kids today are worldly-wise to the point of being cynical. It's really strange being a single parent. I feel as if my responsibility towards Lydia has multiplied. That was one good thing about marriage: we discussed our daughter. Now I make those decisions alone, and I've watched myself become stricter. But I talk with Lydia about everything, and I tell her I love her, and she says she loves me. I also want to check out her boyfriends. I take them fishing to see what kind of people they are. She knows exactly what I'm up to, but she tolerates me. "

"I bet you're a great father," I said, and looked away.

Steven took my hand. "What's wrong, Nina?" he said softly.

"I'm losing my soul in this place."

Giving my hand a slow squeeze, he said, "I trust your spirit. You won't lose that."

"It's strange isn't it?" I said. "How all we've ever shared is sadness and heartache. . . . Hey, do me a favor."

"Name it," he said.

"Tell me about Wyoming. Tell me about the mountains and the smells. Tell me about being a bachelor again."

"Being single's rougher than I ever thought it would be. I've dated a few times, and the women I meet brush me off like lint if they don't get the immediate sense that we're an item. What's worse is,

I don't even know what works. Respect and courtesy don't seem to fit. Dating again after so many years of marriage is just flat-out bizarre.

"They say Wyoming's beautiful," I said.

He brightened. "They speak the truth. I love the mountains, the streams and rivers, the high meadows. Even though Jackson's grown into a rich town, there are still plenty of places where I can get away. And the night sky, when there's no moon, is like diamond dust flung across the heavens. Most of the rivers are clear, and the trout are healthy, and the mountain trails I sneak off to are silent but for the occasional chattering pine squirrel or scolding blue jay."

As Steven was talking, I couldn't stop looking at his hands. They were large and strong and, at the same time, artistic, as if they might be equally at home tying a fly and fretting a guitar. His fingernails were trimmed short, not bitten, and his powerful arms were lean and sinewy. I found myself wanting to be touched by those hands. I must have blushed.

"Okay, Nina, truth or dare," he said, grinning. "What are you thinking?"

"I—I'm sorry," I stammered. "I was listening until my mind wandered off. Can I tell you what the warden asked me?"

"The boss lady? Sure. What'd she say?"

When I had told him the story, he said, "How do you feel about the responsibility?"

"To be honest, mixed. I'm in a funk most of the time. I'm not the type to go around saving people from themselves. Okay, maybe 'save' is too Christian, but to take ten people and try to educate them so they can succeed on the outside seems like a fool's errand."

"I think helping others will be good for you," he said. "It'll get you outside yourself for a while."

"Easy for you to say," I grumped. "What if I fail?"

"You won't fail. Just do what you can. Some of them will absorb some of the information and, hopefully, use it."

I relaxed a little. "Thanks for having confidence in me." We both stopped talking. I could hear the hum of the fluorescent lights overhead. A little girl started crying and broke the awkward silence. "You sure you're okay after the breakup?" I asked.

Steven looked at me, and I could swear his eyes changed color. "I'm good at being alone," he said. "And I love companionship. I just miss not sharing my life—it's that simple."

I felt as if he had echoed my own sentiment. But I couldn't tell him that—not in this environment. "Steven, I spoke to a thief the other day who was telling me how to rob rich people when they take their kids to play soccer or Little League."

"Hah!" he said. "That's the best non sequitur I've heard in a while. If you hadn't stopped me, I might've outwailed that kid over there in the corner."

He laughed again. It was infectious, and I let out a small hiccup of a laugh—so small that I was reminded of just how alien smiling and laughing had become to me.

"Since you've been away, the outside world has changed," he said. "Sometimes I feel like I've been dislodged from the human race. Want to hear something embarrassing? When I go camping, I take my cell phone to call Lydia. Even when I get away, I'm still hooked up."

I smiled. "Okay, how about this: when I sit on a toilet, as many as twenty women might take a peek as they walk by. Little ol' me, who couldn't undress in gym for the whole first year of high school. That's quite a change, don't you think?"

For the rest of the hour, I was so absorbed in what Steven was saying about his daughter and his life on the ranch, I forgot where I was. When the visiting time was over and the guard came to escort him to the door, I hugged him fast. All I could say was, "Thanks."

"I'm with you, Nina, he said. "Read the book and let me know how you liked it."

CHAPTER 18

Each evening after dinner, I would watch June study, then test her on the material. Sometimes it made time go faster. Then one day, her high school equivalency diploma came in the mail. It had taken her almost two years of hard work and study. She had trouble with the math section, but she passed. Along with her exam, she sent the review board an essay, "The Attributes of Great Leadership." This wasn't a part of the test—June just wanted to demonstrate her independent study of leadership. She was fascinated by the influence that a cultural or political leader could have on the minds of people. She told me that both Marilyn Monroe and Martin Luther King Jr. had affected how people thought.

"How's that?" I asked.

"Marilyn Monroe inspired men to think about sex and beauty."

"Getting men to think about sex—there's a no-brainer," I quipped.

She laughed, then continued in a serious tone. "Marilyn also showed women they could be desirable yet genuine. Women sensed that she was the real thing, not a phony."

"So what's the similarity between her and Martin Luther King?" I asked.

"Dr. King asked you to dream. Marilyn Monroe *made* people dream. Both of them appealed to the mind and the imagination. People who speak to the way we think have tremendous influence.

King led blacks into living better lives. Marilyn got people to forget about their everyday lives. She offered escape."

"June," I said, "your speech..."

"Honey, no one's ever asked me to drop my street talk before. You think talking business English like white folks is some big deal. People think we all just a bunch of dumb niggers. It's just a habit for me. Lazy and familiar. In here it doesn't matter, but I get out in nine months. I want a decent job. Time to change."

"You're going to help me with my class?"

"Shit, yes, girl! I'm going to learn what I need to, to get a job. I want you to teach me how to interview. I also want to learn how to use a computer."

"Okay, let's interview now," I said.

"Let's do it." June grinned.

I paused for a second and thought back on what it was like interviewing people for a company eight years ago. "Look me straight in the eye. Answer clearly and concisely. Don't pause too long or hesitate. If you make a mistake, just keep going. Here goes: June, why are you in prison?"

"You serious?"

"In this interview, start with what you know," I said. "Use this role-play to practice. And yes, I'm dead serious."

"I'm in prison because I held up a teenage clerk at a Seven-Eleven store and got ninety-eight dollars."

"Why did you take such a risk?"

"My son, Abel, had pneumonia. My husband was out of work. They laid him off as a machinist when his company cut back. Miserable company!"

"Listen, June, keep your opinions out of the interview. Stay neutral. Don't show emotion unless it's both brief and positive. Otherwise, people will judge you as hostile, and then you're outta there."

"They didn't need to lay him off. The company was doing fine."

"Fine. But look at the big picture. This interview isn't about how unfairly your husband was treated. It's about you playing the game so you have a chance at a decent job. Leave the personal stuff at the door."

She scowled at me. "How do you know so much about this?"

"I used to interview people for the personnel department in a small company. There were some people who would chew gum or twirl their hair during the interview. Some couldn't even look me in the eye."

"I won't chew gum. Hate the stuff anyway. What's your point?"

"It's about creating a good impression. How you speak and look is only the first step, but it matters."

"It's a game, isn't it?" she asked.

"An important game, and both the person looking for work and the interviewer often mislead. There's lots of bullshit. That's why you have to be calm and keep the personal stuff to yourself. People look to make a quick judgment. Your goal is to create a good impression. Go ahead."

June laughed. "You're playing the role like a professional."

"Yeah, well, the warden was serious, so I have to be."

"Fuck the interview—for now, I mean. Thanks, Nina."

It was break time. How strange for me to be the one offering June advice when, only weeks ago, she had been teaching me how to survive. June was staring at me. She seemed eager to finish her story of how she landed in prison.

"I stole the money for medicine. When they discharged my son from the emergency room, they gave me only one week's supply of the medicine he needed to clear his lungs. It was a special antibiotic, very expensive, and we were broke."

She paused and said, "I felt so desperate for my boy; he was only eight. So I took a newspaper and twisted it up and pretended there was a gun inside. I walked into the store like a fool and scared this young gal behind the counter into giving me the money. She got freaked that I had a gun. She looked down, and I could tell she wet her pants."

"Did Abel know you were going to do this?" I asked.

"I never told my husband. He'd never permit it. The man is honest, and so am I. I was just so fucking desperate, I let a really stupid idea take over."

"What happened?"

"I walked out with chump change. They picked me up the next day. The camera got me. The real irony was, one of the cops recognized me from Abel's softball team. Some thief, huh?"

"What did your husband say?" I asked.

"Abel looked at me like he was going to punch me—not that he could ever do such a thing. Then he slammed the table so hard, he hurt his wrist. He was ashamed. He felt it was his fault for not being a good enough provider. His pride was broken. He thought he had let us down. Later, he told me he blamed himself and not me, and just wanted to disappear." June paused and looked down at the floor. Then she shook her head.

"What happened when you were sentenced?" I asked.

"Even though it was my first offense, the judge was hard because I really scared that poor girl half to death. It wasn't armed robbery, but he felt I meant malicious harm by pretending I had a gun. He gave me three years without parole. My public defender didn't protest. When it was time for me to leave the court and come here, Abel and our son, William, watched me being taken away. Abel said, 'I love you,' and I could see his tears. Then little William said, 'I'll miss you, Mama.' My heart just broke into little pieces."

"When did they start allowing conjugal visits?" I asked.

"After two years of good behavior. We're allowed a conjugal every four months. Next Sunday when Abel visits, he's bringing William; they're letting us have a picnic on the lawn. William has only been here twice. I don't like him seeing me in this shit-hole, but my little Willie's growing up—I'm missing some important years.

Abel has a decent job again, and my aunt helps take care of William. He's a good student, a good boy. Anyway, come join us for the picnic. Abel's heard a lot about you, and he'd love to meet you."

"You sure you want me to meet your family?"

"Of course I'm sure! I know, this isn't exactly the greatest place to share them with anyone—except for Edie once in a while. But it's important for them to meet anyone I care about. I used to know all my mama's friends. Now it's time to bring you into the family."

"I'd like that," I told her. We'd been bunkies for all this time, and only now was I learning the most basic things about June. I was puzzled, and it must have shown on my face, because she said, "You wondering why I waited so long to tell you all this, aren't you?"

"Yeah, a little," I said.

"It's about trust, honey—I take my time. So tell me, did I get the job?"

"Can you start tomorrow?" I grinned. "I need a new manager."

"As long as I get full benefits, a good salary, and an hour for lunch, I'm ready."

June squirmed on her cot, then jumped off. She came up to me and stared at me as if I were some exotic fish she had never seen before. With a look of profound gravity, she said, "Have you ever had any joyful time in your life?"

"Sure. I was joyful when I was younger. And there were a few years of happiness when I was married, twelve years ago."

"What happened?" she asked.

"Usual soap opera. He fell in love with another woman. But—and this is important, somehow—she wasn't younger and beautiful with big tits. She was older and fatter than I'll ever be."

June cracked up. "That's weird. Bet she had bucks."

"Bingo. That old, fat bitch was loaded. Anyway, I got over my heartbreak in record time. Once I saw what a greedy fuck he was, I never looked back."

She sat on the edge of my bunk. "You never found another man?"

"More like, another man never found me. I mean, I've dated—never been much for celibacy. I just never met a guy to love."

"We're all in the twilight zone," June said, standing up and rolling back onto the top bunk. "Time for sleep, honey. 'Night."

I closed my eyes, and a strange, bittersweet feeling flooded through me. Steven had visited me only once, yet something about that hour we spent together made me feel both sad and eager. I got a glimpse of how lonely and mechanical I had allowed my life to become. I just lived day to day, without passion, without risk, without love. It had taken prison, an environment far more severe than the one I had created for myself outside, to show me the drab, uniform gray that every stinking day of my life had become. What happened? I was missing life. The years were flowing by while I just went through the motions.

With all my heart, I wanted to wake up with the same curiosity and excitement as a child going to the circus. I wanted something to propel me into feeling alive. I wanted hope and love to be part of my life again. I wanted to dream.

I closed my eyes and conjured an image of a cute boy I knew in high school. Pretending he was making love to me, I stroked myself to ecstasy. Sleep came quickly.

CHAPTER 19

A constant chatter and hum filled the prison, swelling at times to resemble a hive of angry bees. By now, everyone was saying, "Old Doc has the disease." The word spread like a brushfire. Imprisoned women thrive on bad news, maybe because it validates how miserable life can be.

I went into the infirmary, where Doc was helping a sixty-five-year-old woman with a bronchial infection. He was very gentle with the old-timers, many of whom had gotten such inadequate medical attention prison was where they died. Still, everyone knew that Doc would give the best care his limited resources would permit.

When he was finished, he called me into his office and shut the door. "The cancer has just begun to spread," he said. "It's not as bad as I feared, but it's not good, either. I have to continue chemotherapy. The goal is to kill off the diseased—"

"You eating?"

"I need to eat foods that make me regular, like more fruits and vegetables. The doctors want me to eat broccoli because it fights cancer. I always hated broccoli. I'll still eat ribs once every few weeks—a few bones can't hurt. There's this herbalist in town . . . old woman. I never believed in that stuff before, but she's convinced me to take a few herbs for my immune system."

"Take off your shirt," I ordered.

He did, and I saw how frail he had become.

"Lie down on the table."

Once he was facedown with his shirt off, I took some moisturizing cream and rubbed his back and shoulders. His entire body relaxed like an air mattress that's been unplugged. We didn't talk. I had him roll over, and I massaged his chest and shoulders.

When I finished, he got up, put on his shirt, and took a deep breath. "I've been breathing shallow, holding in the tension," he said.

"Christ, Doc, who *wouldn't* be tense?" I said.

"I'm waiting to die. I realized it when you were massaging me. I'm living in anticipation of my death—me, a doctor who deals with people dying all the time, yet I'm not ready to die."

"I'm not ready for you to die, either!"

He sat down on his little round, old-fashioned doctor's stool and just stared off into space. "Would you do that again sometime?" he said. "Just rub this old man?"

"Are you still coming here three times a week?" I asked him.

"I plan to."

"Then it will be my pleasure to massage you three times a week."

"Nina, you're very—"

"You don't need to say it."

"Nina, when you killed that woman in the doctor's office, how did you feel?"

The question caught me by surprise. I chewed on it for a few moments. "Because she and her partner had a gun, and my friend was on the floor bleeding, and I felt threatened. For all I knew, this woman had her own gun, too. It might not have been rational, but I felt like I might be about to die, and I just reacted. I never felt remorseful, sad, or spiritual about it."

"You're changing," he said.

"True enough, Doc. Killing that woman is something that lies buried deep inside me. I know I took a life. I don't feel good about it, but I'm paying for it. It feels like I stepped into a nightmare, and

I'm still in it." I paused. I had been gazing absently at the laminated cutaway chart of a woman's body that hung on the wall. "Do you think I should feel more remorse for taking a life?"

"Don't know," he said.

"Sometimes it still doesn't seem real until I look at the metal bars and taste the food and realize how horrible this place is."

"I didn't mean to confuse you, Nina," he said. "I only wanted—"

"Doc, I don't understand death at all. I can't figure out why my brother had to leave this earth so early. I thought this woman was going to kill me, so I killed her first. Is there something wrong with me that I don't feel sad about that?"

He spun a quarter turn toward me on his little stainless steel chair. "Nina, I'm not some wise old man—just an ordinary old doctor with a new perspective as death starts to call on me. Sometimes everything we do in life seems like a string of accidents and happenstance, but it's not. There's a secret road map we follow. Most people are blind to the directions on their life map."

"What does that have to do with my not feeling remorse?" I asked.

"Forget about her for right now," he said. "I only want you to discover your own road map. Your life and her death are what connected the two of us in this place. That's the part that's significant." He had a tired, sad look on his face. I knew he was experiencing pain.

"You're trying to teach me a lesson," I said.

"Not a lesson. It's just that I want you to choose a direction that's healthy and good for you. Then follow it. You get out of this place in a year. Use the time to chart your new road map; then follow it."

A runner for the warden opened the examination room door. "Warden wants to see you," she said. "Let's go."

I bent over and pecked Doc on the cheek and got a smile out of him, then followed the runner to the warden's inner sanctum.

"Good morning, Warden," I said to her back.

"Nothing good about it. It's raining outside and drab as ever inside."

"Just showing respect, Warden."

"Okay, Miss Manners," she said, turning to face me. "It's time to start the training. We have a room, pencils, and paper for you. Here's the list of eight women, not ten, who are leaving our cozy prison for the real world. I want you to start teaching them tomorrow. Organize them and explain how to apply for a job without sounding like an angry kid from the hood."

"Teach them how to sound white," I said.

"Bury your politics; they bore me. Unless these women are going to interview with a drug dealer looking for a blow job, they'll be as out of place as a bear on a bicycle. Teach them how they need to look and sound so they can work in the straight world. White or black—doesn't matter. Teach them business English. Teach them how to get a legitimate job and stop sucking off the tit of society."

"Yes, Warden," I said.

"Go by what my mother taught me: it's not what you say; it's how you say it."

"Yes, Warden."

CHAPTER 20

The next morning after breakfast, eight women marched into a small room and sat on hard wooden chairs. Harriet, one of three white women, was the first to speak.

"You going to teach us to sing or break bones?" she asked. She smiled and started picking at her nails.

Bobbi, a striking young brunette, said, "Harriet, you plan on being a dumb piece of white trash the rest of your life? Don't diss Nina."

"Nina babe, what are we gonna do here?" a half-black, half-Asian woman asked.

Lin-Yee sometimes helped in the infirmary, and I knew her. I enjoyed her peculiar blend of unabashed arrogance and a dark sense of humor.

I suddenly felt awkward, as if I didn't belong up here in front of eight women. I was never a leader, teacher, or advocate for anything. But these women looked at me with something approaching respect, and they expected me to deliver. In that instant, I decided I wouldn't do a half-assed job. I would give it my best effort, if only because of my commitment to June.

"Okay, ladies," I said. "We're here because Madam Warden asked me to lead a class on how to get a job on the outside when we leave these fine accommodations. The goal is for each of us to find work and stay out of trouble. Any questions?"

"Yeah, what should we call ourselves?" said Eleanor, a close friend of June and Edie. "Let's have a name, like a sports team."

June spoke up. "How about 'the Class of Nine?'"

"I like it," I said. "Be it known henceforward that we are now officially the Class of Nine."

CHAPTER 21

I took out a three-by-five-inch index card on which I had jotted down an actual agenda. I had prepared my opening remarks and just figured I would improvise as we went along.

"Let's start with a couple of rules," I said. First, we all support each other. Nobody gets put down. We want everyone to get out of prison, get a job, and never come back. Second, no whining or complaining. If you like to bitch, leave the anger and tears at the door. Third, take this class as seriously as I do. Even if it's a game to you, play it like you want to win."

Lucinda spoke up. Though she was Latina, she avoided the Mexican gang. She was a loner with a one-note repertoire: angry. That frozen anger had set her face in contours hard as marble. She probably looked that way in her sleep. I thought she might be trouble.

"Yeah, Nina, what's this shit about whining? I *want* to whine. You want me to be on a happy trip?"

"No, Lucinda," I said. I wasn't sure how to handle this, but I couldn't ignore it. "Why are you so pissed off?" I asked.

"Gee, I don't know. Because my scumbag husband used to beat me almost every night? Or because he came home drunk with one of his animal buddies who would fuck a puppy if he had the chance."

"Sounds familiar," said Mary, a light-skinned black woman with dazzling blue eyes.

Lucinda went on: "He wanted to shove a Coke bottle up me in front of his friend. That's when I swore to myself I'd kill him. I couldn't take it anymore."

"If I was around, I would've saved you the trouble, honey," Lin-Yee said.

"Yeah, well, no one was going to help me. I went to the police for a year, and they didn't do shit. Finally, I killed that mean motherfucking piece of garbage. I put half a bottle of sleeping pills in his liquor. When he fell asleep and never woke up, I felt like the doors of hell opened up to let me out and suck him in. I said, 'Bye, baby. I sure hope you burn forever.'"

"Can I say something?" asked Molly, a thirty-something who was so timid, they called her the Mouse.

"Sure, Molly," I said. "What's on your mind?"

"I enjoy stealing. When I worked for my boss, he never tried to touch my body," she said.

"No big surprise there," Harriet said.

Molly looked at Harriet. "I never liked you, you know. You're loud, stupid, and boring."

The room exploded with applause, and I put my hands up in a T, like a ref calling time-out.

"Molly, what's your point about stealing?" I asked.

"Well, this class is about us getting jobs on the outside. When I worked in the bank, I was the assistant to the president. I learned how to rip money off electronically. That means using computers. Maybe I can teach you how to use computers."

"Will you teach me how to steal with a computer?" Lin-Yee asked.

"It's a good idea—I mean the computers, not the stealing," June said.

"I'll ask the warden to get us a computer," I said. "If she does, then your job will be to show us how to use it."

Lucinda stared at me. I knew we had cut her off. It was important to acknowledge her. I didn't know whether she could ever make it on the outside, but I didn't want her to create an atmosphere that would obstruct our purpose.

I walked to the far side of the room, my back to the group. I needed time to digest what I was feeling.

Since being locked up, I had met many women who had killed their abusive husbands. A group of them was being represented by a famous trial lawyer who hoped to reduce their sentences by educating the courts about spousal abuse. In our class of nine, two badly abused women had killed their husbands, and another had tried and failed.

These women, who had killed out of a tortured instinct for survival, seemed different to me from the hardened murderers with no conscience—from women like the Rose, who enjoyed the power that violence conferred.

Bobbi spoke up. "You know, I was always proud of my legs. I had great legs. My husband called me 'doll babe.'"

"What happened?" June asked.

"He changed when he lost his job. He was angry all the time—started slapping me around. The next day, he would always beg for forgiveness. I wasn't sure what to do; I just wanted to believe it would stop."

"Listen, ladies," I interrupted. "We can tell stories only for so long. The warden is on me to get things done."

"Let her finish this one," said Lin-Yee.

"Okay," I said, "but then we move on." I nodded to Bobbi, and she continued.

"One night he came home in a rage. I told him to quiet down and we'd work it out. That's when he hit me. I took a beer bottle and smashed it over his head. Next thing I remember, I was waking up on the kitchen floor. He had knocked me out, then took a cigarette and burned my legs."

"What did you do?" asked Molly.

"I bought a gun from a neighborhood drug dealer—cost me thirty bucks. When he came home that night, I pumped three bullets into him. Sad thing was, he lived." Bobbi's laugh was tinged with self-pity. "Wish I'd a killed that man. Look at this." She lifted her pant legs to show us the ugly burn scars on her calves and thighs.

The mood shifted. Everyone was tense. "Hey, Class of Nine," I said, "we have an opportunity right now. All the pain, abuse, violence, and bullshit can stick to us like chewing gum on a hot day. Or we can go back into the world, work hard, and get out of the hole we're in. Let's learn how to get jobs and make it on the outside! What do you say?"

"God *damn!*" June exclaimed. "You missed your calling. You should be a preacher or a coach."

I smiled. "My point is this: by changing our attitudes, we'll get a job much quicker. An employer is informed from the get-go that we're cons. If they see a lousy attitude, they won't risk hiring us. That means we have to change our attitudes."

"Want me to smile?" Harriet asked.

"What's this shit about business English?" Eleanor asked. "You want us to talk different?"

"Glad you asked, Eleanor. Listen to me without making any judgments. The warden told me she wants the ghetto talk left out during your job interviews."

"What's that mean? You want us to talk white?" Mary asked. "Fuck that!"

"Chill out, Mary!" June said. "This is no bullshit. People who interview us for a job want to hear clear English. Be who you are, but leave the jive, be-bop, slang, cursing, and bad grammar out of your speech." She paused, looking at Mary. "Oh, yeah, and don't chew gum on a job interview."

I looked at June and winked.

CHAPTER 22

"Be-Bop-a-Lula, she's my baby, Be-Bop-a-Lula, she's my baby now, my baby now, my baby now . . ."

"Nina, what's with you?" June said. "I'm not even awake! I haven't heard you sing *ever*. You're acting like something's going on."

I chuckled. "Yeah, I never sing, but I guess 'Be-Bop-a-Lula' is on my mind."

"Babe, you are rarely happy. What's up?"

"The group, I guess. Knowing we're getting out with some small hope of making it on the outside."

June gave a long sigh. "We're almost there," she said. "I can smell breakfast for my boy and my husband. But I don't think about it except when I'm alone at night."

"You think something might set you back?" I asked.

"Nah, not that. I just don't like living in the future when I'm around a bunch of cons. You're doing real good with the group, you know," she said.

"The warden's going to get us an old computer. Molly can teach us to type on it, master the basics."

"You're good with a computer, aren't you?"

"Oh, fair, I guess," I said, "but it's been a while. Better for Molly to show everyone how to use it anyhow."

"From what I hear, the class is into it. Those job interviews we did sure scared the shit out of me. We need to do more interviews. It's hard to break old habits—ones that get you killed here kill you out there, too. Gotta have a safe place to practice."

"Lucinda worries me," I said. "She's always down and angry. I really think she wants to die."

"I heard the Rose is giving her a hard time," June said.

"Why?" I asked.

"She doesn't like you helping a Latina. She's jealous."

"The Rose has juice in here," I replied, puzzled. "People fear her. I'm nothing more than a bug to her. Why would she care?"

"Well, let's see," June said. "She's twisted and cruel. She hears you doing something she can't, and word spreads."

We both stopped talking for a minute. It was a strange silence. I felt pure fear again. Then I thought of Donny. Did he feel calm before the chaos and killing? Or did he feel fear the way I did? A sick feeling engulfed me: The Rose was going to try to kill me.

"You okay?" June asked.

"I don't want trouble with the Rose. I just want to finish my time in this shit house and breathe fresh air again. I want to visit you, Abel, and Willie . . . put this behind me."

"Well, don't let this eat you up," she said. "We'll deal with it."

"Right," I answered, but in my mind's eye, all I could see was Lorraine, her face melted and her life snuffed out by the Rose.

"June, before you fall asleep, tell me why the Rose killed Lorraine."

For a long while, she said nothing. Then she began. "Years ago, Lorraine had a friend in here—Alma, a young black girl who came to her for advice on how to stay alive in this place. Alma walked in the lunchroom and accidentally bumped into the table where the Rose was sitting. That little move spilled coffee on the Rose and gave her an opportunity to build her reputation as a tough-ass."

"What'd she do?" I asked.

"She made up a story that Alma referred to Latina women as

scum. Two days later, the Rose stabbed Alma in the stomach and let her bleed to death."

"Why did Lorraine wait so long to pay her back?"

"Around here, all you have is time. Lorraine was famous for her patience. She wanted to fuck up the Rose by stealing her drugs and turning an addict into her assassin."

"What went wrong?" I asked.

"Lorraine got spotted buying the drugs from the mule, tipping off the Rose that Lorraine was going to make her move. Everyone knew that Lorraine kept away from drugs."

"Couldn't you or Edie do anything?" I asked.

"Lorraine was my good friend, but she was also one stubborn bitch. She felt it was her duty to avenge Alma by herself. She wouldn't let me or Edie help her. She made one mistake, and the Rose wasted no time killing her."

"You really think the Rose is going to make trouble for the group?"

"Not for the entire group. For Lucinda, yes, and my guess is, she'll try to hurt you."

Our cell door swung open, and the day began. I looked at the gray walls merging into the metal doors. Then my eyes wandered down to stare at the hard, cold floors.

After breakfast, I went to the infirmary. Doc was getting thinner. I walked into his office, took off his shirt, and began massaging him.

"Hey Nina," he said, "I hear you're doing well with your class. The warden's talking it up as if she's the ultimate rehabilitation champion."

"It's the women, Doc. They want to make it on the outside; we support each other. But enough of that—how've you been feeling?"

"Don't know what's worse: the cancer or the cure. Keep rubbing that shoulder. *Ooh*, yes. Nina, you have the hands of an angel."

Doc fell asleep. I looked down at his withered body and realized

I truly loved this old man. I covered him with a blanket and left.

The night before, thinking about ways to help the Class of Nine, I came up with a list of qualities that I hated in coworkers. In my various jobs, there had always been someone who complained incessantly—the perpetual whiner who went into endless detail about how the job sucked. I decided to bring this up before turning the class over to Molly for computer training.

"By definition, most of us will get a lousy first job," I said. "Entry level is usually tedious, mind-numbing work. The trick is never to complain in front of a coworker. Even if that person acts like your closest friend, keep your mouth shut, because they can do you in. Just do your job and keep smiling, even when it hurts. Don't complain to anyone near you. Lock your criticism inside, and look at a bad job as a step toward something better."

"Cleaning bathrooms is a disgusting step," said Mary.

"True," I said, "but people who whine on the job get left behind. Then someone else gets the next good opportunity."

"That's right," June said. "You want out of the toilet? Then listen up, girl."

"If you can stand this place, you can certainly tolerate a miserable first job." I paused. "Any questions?"

"Yo, boss." Lin-Yee winked at me. "I can get a job in a massage parlor at night and make five times the money I'll get selling fried chicken with a bunch of teenagers."

"Your twenty-five-dollar blow job'll get you four years as a repeat offender," I said. "Not worth it."

"*Fifty* dollars! Don't insult me." Lin-Yee laughed, ruining her expression of mock indignation. "I know what you're saying, though. I don't want to be back in this hole, but some of this job shit scares me."

"What scares me is not getting work," June said.

"Yeah," said Mary, "why would anyone take a chance on an ex-con black woman?"

"Mary, you're smarter than you think," I replied. "Every small business owner is complaining that people don't care anymore, that they don't work hard. If you work hard, you'll get noticed. I'm telling you, your mental attitude can keep you from coming back to this place."

Molly was looking around. "What's up, Molly?" I asked.

"Where's Lucinda?" she said.

Feeling a sudden tightening in my chest, I said, "Anyone know where Lucinda is?"

"She's in trouble," Mary said. "I heard that in the shower."

"What kind of trouble?" I asked.

Molly, the quiet one, said, "The Rose—that's all I know."

"Anyone know any more about her?"

Molly looked at me and turned white. She was scared. "The Rose is pissed; that's all I heard."

"Okay," I said. "After class, I'm going to find her. Now, we need to continue. Molly has a computer. All we're going to learn today is how to turn it on and type a letter. Everyone has to practice on the computer."

Molly went into exhaustive detail explaining how a computer stored information and how it was used. At first, I worried that she was wasting time, but the group inhaled the information. She had everyone spend five minutes turning the machine on and opening the word-processing program. They each tried typing a letter. Try as I might, I had trouble feeling the group—I was too worried about Lucinda. What was happening with her?

CHAPTER 23

When June finished telling me the horrible news, I wailed like a banshee. The next thing I knew, she was slapping my face.

"Stop it, Nina!" she hissed. "Grab the pillow. Let go of your skin!"

She grabbed my arms and pushed me down on the bed. I had been pinching the skin on my arm so hard that red and white welts appeared. I had lost control and felt only pain, anger, and grief.

"There's nothing you can do, so stop it," June said.

Then I cried—something I hadn't done since Lorraine was killed. Crying in this place seemed weak and meaningless. Eventually, my tear ducts dried up as my anger and hatred solidified into an invisible wall, sealing off all other emotions.

"Tell me again," I said, unable to believe what she had told me.

"They cut off Lucinda's pinkie and index finger on her left hand, and her thumb on her right hand. They left her amputated but bandaged so she wouldn't bleed to death." June looked at me. Her voice dropped into a whisper, as if she feared that saying it out loud would cause me to scream. "When Lucinda got back from Doc's, she slit her throat with a piece of glass. They may as well have pushed her in front of a train. It's no different."

June dampened a washcloth with cold water and rubbed my face. The cold sobered me. Two currents ran through me: detached calm and blood-edged hatred.

"You know for sure the Rose did it?" I finally asked.

"Honey, that motherfucking animal did it. I know because a friend in her gang trades me cigarettes and gossip for lipstick. I get her this dark red shade she puts on at night. She told me the Rose did it because she didn't want Lucinda to get out of here by typing letters from Nina. She has a bug up her ass for you. The way people like the class makes her jealous."

"She coming after me?" I asked.

"What do you think? You've been here long enough." June didn't try to hide her irritation. "We're scared for you."

"That señorita from hell has a strong urge to hurt people," I said. "I think I've lived in enough fear in this place to last a lifetime."

"Edie and Mary and I've been talking about it," she said.

"Yeah? You work out a plan for my salvation?"

"The Rose is hard to get to. It's frustrating," June admitted.

"Another fucking battle I didn't ask for."

"You can't fight her straight on," June warned. "She'll kill you real quick. And she knows you're afraid, which gives her an advantage. We have to change that."

"How?" I asked.

"Don't know yet. But I'll find out soon. You're not alone, girl."

I left June and went to work in the infirmary. Doc wasn't there. When my shift ended, I went to our class.

I walked in to find June, Lin-Yee, Molly, and Edie standing in a huddle. It was odd. Edie had a few more years before she was released, so she had never come to our class. The others were gone.

"What's going on?" I asked.

"Strategy session," said Molly.

"There are several levels to this problem," June said.

"We know the Rose is going to sweat you out with fear for a few days," Edie said. "Then she'll strike. She's feeling like a strong bulldog before the fight. Step one is getting her to feel terrorized. Scare the bitch."

"How?" I asked.

"An older friend of my black daddy told me that in Vietnam there's a snake they called the one-step," Lin-Yee said. "This snake would bite you, and within one step, you were dead. That snake scared the shit out of everyone."

"So?"

"Nina, honey, stop being so fucking abrupt! We need you calm," June reminded me.

"I can get a huge, hairy spider put in her food," Lin-Yee said. "It's not poisonous enough to kill her, but it's so damn ugly it'll scare her."

"Where are you going to get it?" I asked.

"I collect bugs and spiders—I like 'em. They roam this prison like it was heaven. When I find a good spider, I put it in a little box in my cell and feed it roaches. This baby can bite, but that's not the reason we put it in her food. We do it to knock loose some of her confidence. . . . We fuck with her mind." Lin-Yee was beaming with pride.

"Can I speak now?" Molly asked no one in particular.

"Just do it—stop asking!" said Edie.

"I can get a message into the warden's e-mail that the Rose has a shipment of coke in her mattress. The warden will do a search. This will also fuck with her mind."

"Unbelievable. And what do the two of you do?" I asked Edie and June.

"You know we got connections with the guards. We're going to pay a few of them to take the Rose's gang and separate them from her when they come back from the yard after rec time." Edie looked at June and winked.

"Which means you have a window to kill the bitch," Lin-Yee said.

"No fist fight or jab to the throat this time," June said.

"She scares me," I said.

"One of you's going to be dead," Edie said. "You want it to be her or you?"

"I'm a nice girl who happened to kill a murdering junkie," I said. "You may think this stuff comes easy and natural to me, but it doesn't."

"I'm going to help you," Lin-Yee pitched in.

"How?" I moaned.

"We know you can't duke it out with her like you did with the Nazi bitches. So when the guards stop her friends and she's alone in the hallway leading back inside the prison, I'm going to start a fight with her. I'll say hello, walk up to her, and hit her as hard as I can in the face. She'll hit me back, and I'll probably land on the ground. She'll bend over and try to choke me out. When she does, you come from behind with a syringe filled with poison. I can get lye or some weird toxic shit that'll kill her. You take the syringe and push it into her ass or back or arm and get it into her smooth and quick. She'll be dead inside two minutes, and it'll be a better world."

"You in?" June asked.

"Not much choice, is there?" I groaned. "Yeah. I'll do it. Anything for a better world." The joke fell flat. "Afterwards, how do we keep this from the warden?"

"We're going to plant cocaine on her," Edie said. "We have a guard who's going to tell the warden it was a rival gang member. You're covered."

"I love this place," I muttered. "Where else would I thank my friends for helping me kill another human being?"

"Amen!" Edie said.

Walking out of the room, we headed our separate ways, somber with purpose.

CHAPTER 24

I had been writing Steven ever since his visit. He went back to Wyoming and finished out the trout season as a tour guide. His letters were warm and friendly but also had a polite aloofness about them. I found myself thinking about him and visualizing those strong, beautiful hands. He was proud of my class. It wasn't until his most recent letter, when he asked how we liked the computer, that I realized he had helped the warden get it for us. I appreciated how Steven was looking after me. Just knowing he was there made me not feel so isolated. But something else was stirring in me, too: a longing to see his face. *Not now*, I thought.

The upcoming showdown stimulated more conflicting emotions. At times, I felt like the scum of the earth morally. Other times, I felt only an indifference that reminded me of a robot in a sci-fi movie. Between the mood swings, I was frightened, and my heart would periodically race at double time.

I got a long letter from Steven and, even before opening it, sensed a change in his tone. I clutched the envelope against my belly, feeling like a hungry person who delays and heightens the pleasure by smelling the food before taking a bite. Steven was beginning to seep into my emotions, and each time he entered my feeling realm, the sensation became deeper and more filled with longing.

In the infirmary, I asked one of the women to cover for me and went into Doc's office. He was gone, so the place was empty and quiet. I closed the door and started to read.

September 14

Dear Nina,

The tourists are fleeing with sunburns and fish stories. They remind me of fleas jumping off a cat in a warm bath. I love early fall, when you feel the chill and know it's going to get cold and white with snow. There's a preparation for winter that makes me feel alive. I chop wood and tend to the horses. I have a couple of old vets from Desert Storm take care of the other animals and property. These guys were feeling sick and isolated and getting into drugs. The war messed with their brains. Since I took them on, they've become loyal and hardworking. We respect each other, and in many ways, respect was what they needed.

I did something really stupid two weeks ago. I was feeling lonely. Not for Linda the woman, the ex-wife, the person who shared my bed. I was just lonely for a companion—someone familiar to hang out with. At the same time, I blamed myself for the breakup. I was miserable and angry. I don't like getting this angry, because I lose my reasoning.

Anyway, I went into Jackson to get a beer in one of the new fancy bars. I walk in and a few guys are playing pool in the corner, and two guys are shooting darts against the far wall. I buy a beer and walk over to where they're throwing darts. Each guy is about 30 and has his baseball cap on backwards like in a jeans commercial. One guy takes out his cell phone and makes a call. The dart game is on hold while he talks. I tell him to hurry, I want to play darts. Truth is, I don't even like the game.

He tells me to mellow out. I tell him to fuck himself. All the time I'm just feeling miserable and pissed off because I can't stand to lose someone. So his friend tells me, "Mr. Cowboy's in a hurry. Chill out, dude."

I say, "Okay, I'm chilled." He says, "Yahoo, Cowboy Tex." Then he laughs at me. I say, "Cute," and I walk over to him and punch him in the nose. He hits the ground. A few drops of blood fall on his lip. I knew his nose wasn't broken, but I could have hurt him.

Then his friend puts down the cell phone and actually throws a bottle of beer at me. He misses, and it smashes against the table. So I go up to him and grab his wrist. I twist it until he drops to the floor in pain.

The bartender must have called the cops as soon as I got aggressive, because just as I'm about to walk away, my old friend the sheriff walks in and takes me away in handcuffs. He did it for show, because once he gets me in the back of his car and drives off he says, "Steven, you stupid asshole! I don't care if you are just divorced and mad as hell. Maybe we should chip in and get you a punching bag to work it out of your system. You dumb peckerwood, these tourists will go to an expensive lawyer and sue your ass. Now, I'm putting you in jail and letting them know you're locked up. I'll have the doc look at the guy's nose—which you're going to pay for. And with some persuasion and a little luck, we can get 'em out of town without any more trouble."

So here we are, you and I, two law-abiding citizens who don't invite trouble, yet we end up behind bars like a couple of lowlifes. Okay, I realize your situation is a lot more serious than mine. Back here on the range, the sheriff and I grew up together. If anything, he'd cover my ass and protect me. I wish you had it so good. Once he took me in, he never even fingerprinted me or made me sign anything. He basically created a charade to keep me from losing my ass in a lawsuit. Still, he left me in jail overnight, like a father giving tough love to his son.

I must admit, though, hitting that wise-ass made me feel better. Isn't that pathetic? I'm lonely and pissed about being single again, and I revert to stupid raw aggression. So much for the power of reason. Actually, I knew from the days when I got back from the desert, after Donny got killed, that I had to talk to someone. When I ran into Ellen, an old family friend who had just become a psychologist, I was just a blown-away kid, shell-shocked from the war. Eagle Heart, my Indian teacher, spent months working with me. One day I told him about Ellen, and he persuaded me to go talk to her. So I did. She listened to me talk about the war and my rage and offered genuine compassion. She had me pay her a token ten dollars per session. She insisted that I be on time and take it seriously. We did that for about five months, until I realized I needed to rejoin the human race.

It's a bit embarrassing to say, but I went back to see her after this bar incident. It turns out my divorce is kicking up feelings of loss that connect to Donny. I never thought therapy was for real, but if I hadn't talked with her, I would never have made sense of the feelings bouncing around inside me.

When someone you care about leaves suddenly, the connection snaps back at you like a broken bungee cord. The connection is broken. That sense of broken connection first occurred when Donny died in my arms. I felt like I had lost a limb. Eagle Heart helped me deal with the tremendous sense of loneliness from my broken link to Donny. He taught me how the Indians revere the memory of the dead. They take those connections, those lines, and extend them into a ceremony. They prolong the meaning of relationships and allow them to continue in a spiritual realm. Regardless of how embarrassed I feel telling you these thoughts, I want you to know that when I talk with you like this, and when I see you, I feel a powerful connection. It's easy for me to talk to you. I don't feel I'm risking, because you already accept me. I think about you more and more, and not because I'm unhappy. I'm only unhappy some of the time. I can't articulate it with the same intensity that I feel it, but I care about you. Take care in your dungeon, Nina. Time is a bullet train, and you'll be out soon.

Steven

CHAPTER 25

The next day, Doc was back in the infirmary, looking shrunken, old, and sad. Watching him slowly die made me morose; then the gloom gave way to anger. I wanted to scream, *Don't die!*

Doc looked at me with those piercing gray eyes and smiled. "I don't have much longer," he said. "You and I have come a long way. We're real friends now."

The sadness swept over me, and I said, "Hey, Doc, let me give you a rub."

"Be real gentle. My entire torso feels like it was dunked in a french fry cooker. I'm on fire."

As I started to rub him, he said, "Nina, why the hell can't you stay out of trouble? Everyone in this infirmary is focused on you like they were staring at a dancing cobra. They all like and respect you, and they want to help, but they're afraid for you."

"Y'know, Doc," I said, gently kneading the gaunt shoulders, "I once had a friend who told me she was born under a lucky star. She said only good things happened to her."

"Lemme guess—she choked on blueberry pie and died." Doc chuckled.

"Close. She fell off a horse, landed on her head, and never woke up."

"Gee, that's a fun story, Nina! Got any more?"

"Doc, I need some luck real bad," I said. "I'm tired of being afraid. It's strangling me. I feel like a cow with a bell around my neck that only attracts trouble."

He gave a little, gasping laugh. "If it turns out there's anything on the other side after I die—you know, if we still have awareness—I'll miss you more than anyone I know. When you pray for me, I'm going to pray back that your cowbell's removed and you find some peace. Just remember what I once told you: find your center of gravity, your purpose, and follow it. The lucky star will be there for you."

"Go to sleep, Doc," I said. And I put a blanket over his skinny shoulders and prayed for him.

CHAPTER 26

That night, June insisted that we hit the chow line early. We each got our ladleful of brown stew that smelled like three-day-old catfish. June led me to a table in the back, where Edie and Lin-Yee were already sitting down.

"Keep your head down but eyes open," Edie said.

About ten minutes into the meal, the Rose walked in with her entourage. In another time and place, I would have seen her as beautiful. But all I noticed was her arrogance. She didn't walk to the food line; she strutted like a prizefighter, dancing and gliding as if she had a cushion of air between her and the floor. It was quite a show.

She took her tray, got her food, and chose a table. Everyone in her group waited for her to sit first, as if she were some kind of royalty. Lin-Yee clamped down on my thigh under the table, looking like an eager child who couldn't contain her anticipation. June's eyes darted furtively back and forth.

Suddenly, the Rose shrieked, jumped up, and flung her tray on the floor. Then, with her fork, she flipped the biggest, hairiest spider I had ever seen from her plate onto the floor and stomped it. We all looked down, as if suddenly fascinated by the gravy on our plates. When our eyes came back up, the Rose glowered in our direction. Then she calmly walked out of the mess hall.

The four of us took a deep breath and let out a sigh of relief.

Edie gulped some air and said, "That asshole got scared. She saw those big ugly, hairy spider legs in her food and nearly shit in her pants."

We laughed.

June looked at Lin-Yee. "Good job, girl. Real good job."

My heart was racing, and I could feel the adrenaline starting to surge through my body. I knew I had to calm down. As if reading my mind, June said, "Breathe deep and slow. That's all you can do to slow it down."

I took a deep breath and looked at June. She winked at me.

"Tomorrow's the big day," Lin-Yee said. "The guards are going to separate the Rose from her gang. Tomorrow we settle things."

"Is the syringe ready?" I asked.

"Okay, I'm not supposed to tell you this," she said. "Doc told me about this medicine. In a large dose, it mimics a person having a heart attack—in other words, it'll kill you if you take much. Doc innocently mentioned where he keeps it, and by coincidence, that section of the medicine cabinet was unlocked. So there's no need to use lye—we got something better."

I must have gone pale.

"Nina, keep breathing," Edie said. "Don't you freeze up on me!"

Molly came in and sat quietly at our table. She turned to us with a sly little grin on her face. I could see how she must have enjoyed stealing money electronically.

"My best friend on the outside just sent the warden an e-mail," she said. "Her address is secret, but I got hold of it. The e-mail tells of a certain bag of coke in the Rose's cell."

"Nina, the Rose is smart," June said. "She'll know all this shit happening to her means you're not acting alone. In some small way, that'll keep her off balance—it's the best we could do."

Edie whispered, "Tomorrow the señorita will meet her maker. I hope she burns in hell."

CHAPTER 27

The smell of tension permeated our prison yard. Everyone smoked, talked, and stared at the grass as if they were watching frogs copulate. Many women were hanging out only within their own ethnic group. To keep conflict and violence to a minimum, some groups often made political deals not to hang out near each other. The Aryans and blacks had worked out an accommodation: they alternated days for which side of the field they used. In my time here, I had already seen one agreement break down between a Mexican group and some whites, which resulted in one death.

Some women exercised and kept in shape, but most turned into chubbettes from the starchy food, or maybe they were fat to begin with. Once women prisoners got overweight, they rarely made an effort to slim down. It always surprised me how heterosexual women could leer at certain women with big, firm breasts and thin waists every bit as intently as gawking, horny men.

I usually stayed in a remote corner of the yard with Edie, June, Lin-Yee, and a few other women. Lin-Yee had juice with the Asians, some of whom I worked with in the infirmary. The black gang respected and liked Edie and June, and after my fight with the Needle, the Aryans left me alone. What fragile peace existed would soon be shattered, though, and everybody felt it.

My heart was racing, yet I felt an inner calm that seemed to be my new approach to battle. I had no impulse to run from the coming fight.

I remembered Edie's words as if they were tattooed on my arm: "Honey, it's either you or her. Make sure it's her—you're doing it for you and for Lucinda."

The whistle blew, and the inmates walked back inside. In the corner where the Mexicans always made their entrance, three guards moved in. To my surprise, one guard was white, one black, and the third Latina. I had assumed that Edie and June had pull only with the sisters, and I felt oddly gratified to know they had diversified their bribes.

To reenter the bowels of the prison from the yard, we had to pass through a well-lit concrete-lined tunnel, whose walls were curved rather than square. The tunnel enclosed all of us before we reached the heavy barred door into the prison. Just as the Rose's girls came into the tunnel, the three guards separated them from their leader.

"*Señorita puta*, move on!" bellowed the Latina guard, brandishing a can of mace in her right hand and a nightstick in her left.

Lin-Yee was already in position at the far end of the tunnel.

The Rose must have known she was in trouble, yet she moved forward as if she were a soccer player about to kick a goal. Edie and June had patted my ass for good luck, and I was on my way. As I approached the tunnel, the guards led the Rose's crew back into the yard, toward a separate entrance on the other side. Just as I was about to step inside, an old lifer walked up to me and palmed a glass syringe into my hand and disappeared around a corner.

I kept walking until I saw Lin-Yee and the Rose. Blood was pulsating in my ears, like a big, soft drum pounding in the distance.

I was maybe ten feet from the Rose when Lin-Yee said, "Yo, Rose bitch. I have some important news about an attempt on your life." Then she walked up to the Rose and hit her in the jaw with everything she had.

The Rose treated the punch like a mosquito bite, rubbing her cheek more in annoyance than in pain. Then, with the grace of a cat, she darted up to Lin-Yee, who bravely stood her ground. With both hands, and the Rose grabbed Lin-Yee by the collar and pushed her so hard, Lin-Yee collapsed. Then, with alarming speed, the Rose was on top of her, hands at her throat. Lin-Yee gasped and hacked and began to go blue. She was about to die.

An instant later, I was behind the Rose and plunging the syringe into her ass. It went in up to the hilt, a good inch or more into her flesh.

"*Hija de la chingada*—what the *fuck* . . . !" the Rose bellowed, loosing her grip on Lin-Yee's throat and turning to look at me. But before she could rise, the first spasm rippled through her. Then a stronger tremor hit, and her eyelids fluttered as she rolled off Lin-Yee. She looked dead.

Lin-Yee crawled out from under her larger attacker, reached into her underwear, and came up with the bag of cocaine. Coughing and gasping, she rubbed her throat and muttered, "Shit!" Then she slipped the coke into the Rose's bra, grabbed me and the syringe, and hustled me off to the prison entrance. As we entered, we heard a whistle and knew that the guards were right on time.

I went to the bathroom and vomited, trembling as if I had been caught naked in a snowstorm. My body didn't stop shaking for almost an hour.

Back in the classroom, all five of us were happy the Rose was dead, but we couldn't show it. Instead of high-fiving and hugging, we acted like strangers to each other. Even June walked away from me and struck up a conversation with Bobbi. I felt like a sick soul . . . a killer.

A runner came to the classroom and gave me a message. I was needed in the infirmary. I thought for sure I would be busted for murdering the Rose.

When I arrived, Doc called me into the little emergency room. The Rose was stretched out on the hard metal table, with IV feeds flowing into both arms. I saw her chest move and knew she was alive and breathing. How could this be? I had injected the full contents of the syringe into her.

"Did you really think I'd let you kill her, Nina?" Doc asked.

I was flummoxed. "What do you mean?" I asked.

"Your archenemy has a high dosage of liquid vitamins and Valium in her system. I didn't want her dead—not that she doesn't deserve a long stay in hell. But there was no way I'd let you kill again, even if it was in self-defense. This is my last gift to you. This is how we get the cowbell off your neck."

"You planned this alone?" I asked.

"This old man still has a move or two in him—remember that."

"What happens now?"

"I spoke to the warden and told her about finding cocaine on the Rose. She's waiting for me to release her so she can be shipped to a maximum-security prison for violent and out-of-control prisoners. Your lovely friend is finished in this house of redemption."

"Does anyone know she's alive?" I asked.

"Of course! I have six inmates spreading the news that the Rose is alive and about to be shipped to maximum security."

I sat down and laughed so loud that Doc had to put his hand over my mouth. I felt genuine joy for the first time in years.

"No more cowbell, then?" I asked.

"No more cowbell."

"Doc, I love you so much," I said. "I'll always be grateful for what you did."

"Time to get back to your class and resume your role as teacher," he said. "See you tomorrow for my rub."

I looked at the Rose for the last time. Then I gave her the finger and said, "For Lucinda, you miserable fuck." And I walked out.

CHAPTER 28

I felt as if I had just returned from the dead. I'd gotten an unexpected dispensation. Doc knew that if I had killed the Rose, I would never recover psychologically. Taking a life, even one as worthless as hers, would have tormented me for the rest of my life.

I didn't quite know the purpose of life, especially my own, but being in prison was my constant reminder that life is not mine to take away. Doc had tricked me, but I was actually elated that my enemy had survived.

Doc told me my cowbell had been removed. That meant I was free to discover a new life. I had no idea what starting over would feel like in the world I was about to enter, but I was eager to find out.

CHAPTER 29

The elation didn't last. My mood shifted. I didn't feel morose or despondent, but I wasn't happy, either. I felt as if I were in a fog of emotional indifference. In some ways, I was asleep again, blithely jaywalking through life as I had in my previous existence, when I went to work, came home, watched TV, and went to bed, day after day. But feeling numb beat being gripped by claustrophobic fear and depression.

Another gray day began. After lunch, the guard said I had a visitor. It was so unexpected, I thought it must be a mistake. Instead of the usual visiting room, I was taken to a small room of cinder block painted the color of cigarette ash. There was a table and two chairs, and a guard stood by the door, discreetly out of easy hearing range.

In walked Steven, with a huge grin on his face. I was shocked to see him—his last letter hadn't mentioned anything about coming down to visit. I couldn't smile back. I was delighted to see him, but it felt as if someone had put Krazy Glue on my lips, preventing me from opening my mouth. He walked over and touched me on the shoulder. I noticed those strong, supple hands again.

"I wanted to surprise you," he said.

"Why?" I asked.

"I've been thinking about you, Nina."

I didn't know how to respond, so I just stood there like a lump.

"What's wrong?" he asked. "Aren't you at least a little bit glad to see me?" That grin again.

"How's Lydia?" I said.

"You might find this strange, but she wants to meet you. She thinks you're a cool person, enduring this shit and fighting for your life."

"I'm a prison-babe role model," I joked. "What does she think about the fact that I killed somebody?"

"You were being robbed. Your friend was shot and bleeding on the floor. You fought back; she died. They put you in this place for involuntary manslaughter. My daughter has no moral problems with that." He peered into my eyes. "Do you?"

"Sometimes knowing I killed another human being makes me feel dirty inside," I said.

"You did what you had to. For that woman to come into your office to steal drugs, with an accomplice who used a gun, means she knew the risks or was too stupid to care. You reacted to the threat. Killing someone will live with you, but you can make peace with what you did. Spiritually, you can heal the wounds. I'm not a moral judge, but I know you're not a killer."

"Thanks, Steven," I said. "That means something."

"I talk to my daughter about you. She listens and wonders why I keep thinking about you. Finally, she was sitting there, legs crossed like someone meditating on life, and she said, 'Dad, I want to meet Nina. She means a lot to you. Would you introduce us? Going to a prison doesn't scare me.'"

"No disrespect for your little angel, Steven, but it scares the shit out of me."

"You having more trouble?" he asked.

"Yeah, you might say—if almost killing another psycho woman qualifies as 'more trouble.'"

"Jeez, what happened?"

I told him about the Rose. When I was done, he reached out

and held my hand. His touch made me quiver. Tears rolled down my cheek. He reached into his pocket and took out a tissue and gently wiped my tears. I felt like a child again, when my dad would hold a handkerchief and tell me to blow my nose. I smiled for the first time since Steven arrived.

Reaching over, he pulled a quarter out of my ear. It was such a corny old trick, but it worked. I cracked up, my laughter bouncing off the concrete walls. The guard looked at me and put her thumb up in the air, then held her index finger over her mouth. She didn't want me to attract attention.

Steven said, "I'm in town to talk with an ad agency about a photography job. They want to create an image of ordinary people and get away from their earlier glam ads of leading-edge models and stars. Both the ad agency and the client like my photos, especially some of my outdoor shots using neighbors and friends."

"I don't even know what's happening out there in the big world," I said. "In here we watch TV, and the stories all seem so distant and abstract."

"The world is moving fast," he said. "Jackson Hole's beautiful, but it's getting congested in the summer with tourists, art galleries, and espresso shops. Fortunately, my ranch is in a wilderness area that hasn't been invaded—yet, anyway. Because of my photography work, I need to stay on top of the new technology. I now take pictures digitally so I can send them instantly to the agency. I have a digital cell phone and digital camera hooked up to a computer. Seems that the digital world is hooked up to everything except our thoughts—and that's just a matter of time."

"Gee, you'd think I was found frozen in the snow and resuscitated after a couple of centuries went by," I said.

Steven laughed. "Sometimes I prefer the old ways. Too many people relate better to a computer then to another human being— seems like a bad tradeoff."

"Steven, this cave woman wants to know why you're suddenly

visiting me."

"Well, Nina, this cowboy dude has a lot on his mind," he said, suddenly earnest. "Permission to get personal?"

"Oh, my, I feel it coming," I said. "Talk to me."

Steven took a long breath and gazed into my eyes. I couldn't look away, so I just took a deep breath and looked back. My nervousness vanished. I was calm, receptive.

"We take for granted the very real bond we shared that night while praying for Donny," he said. "We joined in a sad spiritual moment to acknowledge the loss of my best friend and your brother."

"If you hadn't been there with my mom and dad that night to share the grief, I wouldn't have made it," I said. "Here in prison, when I'm awake at night with my mind bouncing off the walls, I think about us saying that beautiful prayer. I remember how you held my fragile mom and dad and hugged them." I wiped my tears with my sleeve and looked away.

In reply, he took my hand and rubbed his thumb gently across the knuckles. Then he said, "After the war, I came back to my ranch in Wyoming, and part of me was broken inside. Eagle Heart insisted I spend time with him. He wouldn't let me be alone except when we went into the mountains. Then he led me in some rituals where I talked with the dead. He helped me glue myself back together. Later I got married, had a baby girl, and got back to my life. With you and me, Nina, our friendship started out vague and distant. We each had our own voyage to lead."

"As for me," I said, "if there's one lesson I've learned from this house of stench, it's how ordinary I had become. It's as if I had stopped living for myself. Something about this fear-driven environment has made me realize that a part of me was already dead inside when I got here. Do you think, in some strange way, it was because of losing Donny?"

"A wiser person than I will have to answer that," he said. "I suspect you already know the answer. But you *aren't* ordinary, and you aren't dying inside. You convey courage, and you have so much untapped warmth. You have an old-fashioned goodness, Nina."

"It's hard to hear those words without arguing, but I'll accept them," I said. "Doc is my wise old teacher. As he nears death, he always reminds me that I can choose to be happy. I can choose to have a life without feeling burdened with so much unhappiness. With Doc, I've found a wise friend in my life."

"Yeah. Eagle Heart offers me similar lessons. It seems as we get older, the choices we make become the critical ingredients for living."

"How much time do we have left in this visit?" I asked.

"Not long. Nina, I have very strong feelings for you. I want to know you outside this prison. And that time isn't far away. I want you to think about me and what I'm telling you. I care very much about you. I want us to become something together."

Steven turned around and motioned to the guard that he was ready. Then he bent down and gave me a gentle kiss on the cheek and left me to ponder that small gesture. It was not just affection; it was an invitation. I could feel what he was saying, and it made me cry.

CHAPTER 30

The class was fun. We knew our time in prison was nearing an end. Molly got braver and spoke up more, and the other women started to respect her. Harriet, too, showed more confidence. June took diction so seriously, she sounded like Maya Angelou reciting a poem. Lin-Yee maintained her usual cocky stance, but underneath the surface she was kind and caring.

Even Mary was changing. As soon as she started to blame everyone for her life's misery, the group put their hands over their ears. She was still convinced that the world had done her wrong, but we interrupted the whining habit.

The other two white women, Harriet and Bobbi, were terrified of life on the outside. Being a prisoner was such a shifting, life-altering experience that the outside seemed like a parallel universe in a science-fiction movie. Most people in here had few skills to begin with, and leaving prison brought to the surface each woman's sense of being a misfit. It made them wonder how they could ever make it out there.

We tried to remind each other to speak simple, clear English, have a positive attitude, and make every job count. We would talk about finding work, getting laid, meeting someone nice, having a shower all by ourselves. We tried to be optimistic and hopeful, but these women had never felt optimism, and hope was something they left for their heroines on the afternoon soaps.

Doc called for me a month before my release. He asked if I would rub his back. I took off his shirt, put moisturizer on my hands, and began massaging his bony shoulders.

Normally, he was quiet during the rubs, but he must have felt talkative. "One of the girls tells me you're different since . . . what's his name? Oh, yeah, since *Steven* visited. I'm told you're quiet and moody in a different way. Is that true, what they're saying?"

"Doc, if I farted and it sounded different, you'd know about it. Yes, I feel different, but I can't put it into words."

"Wasn't this man wounded when your brother was killed?" he asked.

"Yeah, he's the one I told you about."

"I know nothing has touched you as deeply as losing your brother, Nina. Steven was part of that experience. You're already exposed to each other in some important way."

"What are you getting at, dear Doctor?"

"We both know I'm not going to be around this nuthouse planet much longer, so I want to leave you with a thought that has been pondered forever."

"Which is . . . ?"

"Which is life's most worthwhile activity." Doc lingered with the thought, like a pitcher holding the ball before the windup. "In my opinion, to love and be loved is the most important thing we can do. Everything else is a walk-through. Love is the theme of almost every country song and soap opera, and the cause of most heartache and pain. Love is the big enchilada. Love makes our crazy ride through life worthwhile."

He paused, and I said, "Tell me more about that."

"I'm talking about good love, real love, enjoyable love," Doc said. "I'm talking about love that pumps the heart full of enough energy to care about someone besides yourself. I'm talking about love that makes you feel more complete than you did before. I'm talking about love that makes God applaud."

"Why are you telling me this now?" I asked.

"Because if you have even the slightest chance of loving and being loved, I want you to grab on and never let go. If this man cares about you, and there's the smallest opportunity that you can care in return and make a relationship work, I want you to treat it like it's the most precious thing ever."

I kissed his head. "You're like my granddad. You've given me so much..."

"I *feel* like your granddad. When you start to die, there's an important question that hovers above you like a rain cloud."

"Go on. You're rolling."

"The thought goes something like this: 'Old man, what did you do in your life that was worthwhile?' A lot of the time I accomplished nothing meaningful. But with you, Nina, I did something good. That's because I believe in you. All I ask is that you grab your second chance and try hard to make it work—nothing more than that."

"I will, Doc," I said. "I promise."

I continued to rub him until he fell asleep. Then I covered him with a blanket, patted him, and left.

About an hour after dinner, I was called into the warden's office. She wasn't wearing her usual scowl. She looked genuinely sad.

"Nina, Doc died about twenty minutes ago. I wanted to tell you. The cancer had traveled to his liver. He had to be in a lot more pain then he let on."

"But... I was just with him," I stammered, my lip quivering.

"I know. Listen, Nina, I've known about his sex barter for a long time. Not that I approved, but in a strange way, he helped keep this prison from exploding. I also know he valued your friendship."

I started to cry. At first I felt some of the same searing emptiness I had felt when they told me Donny was dead. I was determined to get the hell out of this shit-hole and make a life for myself on the outside. I owed Doc an effort worthy of his love and friendship. This determination felt new and strong, and it gave me hope.

"Would you plan a small memorial for Doc with the chaplain?" she asked. "He mattered to a lot of people, including me. Plan something short, simple, and tasteful." Then she gestured for me to leave.

Word of Doc's death spread immediately. I met with June's friend Lizzie, who led the choir in the prison church. I asked her to sing a gospel hymn. She told me she understood exactly what I wanted. "Honey, I'll make you cry and make you feel joy for the old man."

That Sunday we had Doc's memorial. The choir sang "Amazing Grace." Then I got up, and everyone was quiet.

I said, "We're behind bars and feel how harsh life is. Many of you have transferred in from other prisons, where they wouldn't believe you if you were sick. Often you had to beg for medical treatment, and even then you might not get it."

Several voices yelled out, "Yeah, that's right!"

"Doc never turned anyone away if they were hurting. He didn't humiliate us for wanting medical help. He was gentle and treated us with dignity. He didn't play race games. He had friends in every group. He loved eating ribs, and often you could smell them on his clothes where he'd spilled the sauce. Doc encouraged me to find something deep inside myself that's good and decent. He helped heal my soul the same way he'd heal a broken bone. It's hard to keep a warm heart in this place. Regardless, I ask every one of you to hold him dear in your hearts. He represented the best in all of us, and we should remember him with love."

Edie stood up and yelled, "Amen!" The other women, and even two of the guards, echoed it. I sat down. The memorial was over. Doc was gone.

CHAPTER 31

"Abel and Willie are so excited they can't stand it!" June said.

"How you holding up?" I asked.

"Can't put it into words—too nervous. They'll be at the gate in two hours."

"Tell me for the last time, where did Abel move to?"

"He moved us to Modesto. He got a good job as a manager in a coffee company. He has responsibility, and they like him. Willie's already in eighth grade. Abel says the school is good. Modesto used to be a little farm town, but it's growing as people escape the city."

"You promise to have me over?"

"Honey, I can't *wait* to have you over. Be nice to invite you and your friend, if you get my drift."

June looked like the black goddess I first saw when I looked into those beautiful dark eyes. She laughed and said, "What you looking at?"

"You're as beautiful as ever," I said.

We both shook our heads. "It's been a long ride," she said.

Edie and I were the last to hug June before she walked out. And when she was gone, it hit me just how attached we had become. I'd never had a friend like her: smart, tough, and caring. June had shown me how to compose myself and fight insanity. Now there wasn't anyone to talk to when the lights went out.

So instead, I reflected, spent time scanning my memories, and realized that my view on life was changing. I could be honest and critical with myself rather than explain and excuse and bullshit my way through. I also recognized that I lacked self-esteem when it came to being in a relationship. The idea of having a relationship with Steven seemed as remote as wrestling crocodiles. I remembered an old Willie Nelson song where he says, "I never thought I'd be in love again." Could I love Steven? Was it as simple as getting on a bicycle and remembering how to peddle? Love had seemed so out of reach for so long. My heart felt dormant, atrophied, like a muscle that hasn't been used for so long it's forgotten how to work. And I'd lost touch with my body—fifteen pounds heavier from eating starchy food and lazing around when I could be exercising. I was determined to shed the weight and begin my new life.

CHAPTER 32

Six weeks had passed since Steven visited. He came riding in on a white horse and talking about how deeply he cared about me. At first, I just didn't believe I was worthy of anyone's caring. My life was built around deep insecurities. I didn't want to analyze myself to death, and I didn't have the luxury of talking with a therapist, but Doc had been a therapist of sorts. More like shock therapy, I suppose. He reminded me what was good about me. It was as if, by his kindness, he had held up a mirror and made me look into the reflection and find something decent and valuable about myself. Doc left me with a lesson about life, and the lesson was all about love—that to love and be loved was what made the struggle worthwhile. So in honor of Doc, I decided to change my thinking and take his last words to heart. Without those words boring into my soul, I might well never have considered the meaning of love.

I thought about Steven and smiled at the memory of his hands, his honesty and humor, his core of strength and kindness. It dawned on me that I loved him, had loved him ever since we first met in Milwaukee and prayed together. Even so, I just never considered that my feelings for him could or would translate into anything more than a distant friendship.

Steven told me that some Native Americans refer to God as the Great Mystery. Sitting here deciding to write to Steven seemed part of that great mystery. It was now time to respond and meet his affection with a boldness that would have been alien to the pre-prison Nina. It was my time to be brave and honor both Doc and Donny by being forthright with my true feelings. For the first time in my life, I felt a new freedom. And with that spark of aliveness in my heart, I began to write:

Dear Steven,

I get out in five weeks. Time is crawling by right now, but five weeks is not very far away. It took Doc's final words before he died, his talk about love, for me to digest your last visit and to say this to you. I want to crawl out of my cave and tell you the truth.

I feel nervous, as if I were sitting on a train, waiting for it to leave the station and take me on a new journey.

Before writing another word, I studied my nails, stared at the gray walls, looked down at the floor and then back to the paper.

So here goes: I care about you so very much, and it frightens me to death to tell you this. I love you. What can we do about this? Please let me know soon.
I hope you and Lydia are well.

Yours,
Nina

CHAPTER 33

When Steven's reply to my letter came two days later by overnight FedEx express, it completely changed my sense of time. In prison, every dreary day dripped into the next at glacial speed. Work and meals were mechanized in lockstep with the clock. But Steven's lightning response, coupled with the fact that I would be leaving soon, condensed the past, present, and future into a single tick of the clock.

I was preparing myself to leave but didn't have a definite plan. This was the most important juncture of my life, and I was unsure which mountain pass I would take. And yet, this didn't scare me as it would have in the past. Somehow, I knew that whichever route I took in life, my choice would work out. The only certainty I had about my departure from this place was that I' would fly to Milwaukee and visit my parents. My dad had just turned eighty, and my mother was seventy-six. Neither was ill beyond the usual complaints of aching bones and arthritis, but I wanted to spend time with them. Also, they needed to know I was okay.

I was sweating, and my stomach felt fluttery. I could almost hear June saying, "Get on with it!" So I opened the letter.

Dear Nina,

I'm nervous about all this, too. I was walking in circles until Lydia did for me what I've always done for her. She took me horseback riding in a meadow filled with purple wildflowers. She took out the picnic basket and spread everything on a blanket, and then she told me, "Dad, you're driving yourself—and me—crazy. Tell me everything."

When I was done talking to my ageless daughter, I had a plan. It's a plan based on the premise that we can love each other and have a life together. That makes me tremble.

Here's the plan: I pick you up when you get out next month. We go to San Francisco, where I've booked separate rooms for us at the Fairmont Hotel. The next day, I take you to the airport and you fly to Milwaukee and visit your parents.

I need about three days in the city to finalize my ad campaign and the photo shoot for the agency. When I'm done, I'll fly to Milwaukee. I want to see your parents for myself and for Donny, as well as to be with you. I'll stay in Milwaukee for two days and then fly back to Wyoming.

When you're ready to leave Milwaukee, fly to Jackson, where Lydia and I will pick you up at the airport and take you to our ranch. There's a real nice separate cabin with a kitchen, wood-burning stove, and TV. You can stay there while we sort things out. I don't have anything fancy to offer—just old-fashioned Wyoming hospitality, the way it used to be.

I promise not to rush things. We can date and get to know each other. I'll respect your privacy and autonomy as much as possible. Lydia will not be a creepy, crappy, annoying kid—she doesn't have it in her. She's still as excited as ever to be with you. Her attitude has helped me, and I know you'll like her. I feel that this can work. Please give us a chance.

I'll support you in whatever choices you make. I will be at the *gate when you walk out of the snake's belly. Please think about us. See you soon.*

Steven

I put down the letter and cried. For the first time in a long time, I felt desired.

CHAPTER 34

Two months had passed since June left, and now it was my turn to leave the hell of prison. Martha, the guard who first warned me about prison life, escorted me from my room to see the warden. The warden had a changed look, like a lonely lady who hung out in bars talking to herself. I knew she could have treated me a lot more harshly. Out of self-interest, she had extended me favors. Yet I couldn't get over how she symbolized the rampant lack of humanity in this place. She had made decisions that determined my fate and controlled my life, but now I no longer dreaded her as an authority figure. She was old, over, used up.

"I predict that four from your class will make it and four will return," she said.

"I predict they all walk out of this sewer and never look back."

"Cute, Nina. Leave now; I have nothing more to say to you."

"Good-bye, Warden. Hope you make it to Sacramento." I turned and walked away.

Before leaving, I gave my friends a kiss. Lin-Yee grabbed my ass and pinched me, then gave me a hug. Edie and I looked at each other. I touched her cheek. She said, "You did good, girl! Real good." I was about to thank her when she laughed out loud. "Don't you think for one second your little whitebread ass could have made it without Edie coaching you."

I smiled. "No way I'd have made it without you." Her lips tightened, and a tear rolled down. I knew she would have a rough time adjusting without her best friends: Lorraine, June, and me.

"The time will go fast," I said.

"It'll go slow as shit, and you know it."

"I love you, Edie, and I'll never forget what you did for me. I'll write you, I promise."

Martha took me to pick up my valuables, and I signed my release, picked up the bag with my few belongings, and didn't look back. I heard the jeers and shouts and catcalls of prison women for the last time.

CHAPTER 35

I knew that Steven would be there to pick me up, and I walked out the door feeling shy and a little scared. But I didn't have long to think about it. He walked over to me and lifted my arms up over his shoulders. At first he hugged me very gently. My body was limp as a cushion. Then, without thought, both my arms wrapped around him and wouldn't let go. He crushed me to him, and I understood the cliché of having my breath melt away. We embraced for a long time.

"Welcome to the real world," he said.

"Thanks for getting me."

We drove north to San Francisco, talking even through the stops for food and gas. It was an easy, relaxed talk, as if not a week had passed since we met long ago, when both of us were not quite twenty. At times he would crack a joke, and we would laugh. Sometimes he would tell me something sad, and I could feel what he was saying. It was the most blissful ride I ever had.

Steven and I arrived in San Francisco in the late afternoon. He took us to the Fairmont on Russian Hill, a big, pompous old hotel that made me feel self-conscious. It seemed overly extravagant to be spending so much money after I had just spent two and a half years in a tiny cell. Steven told me he expensed it to the ad agency, and he thought the rich and gaudy surroundings were the perfect contrast to prison. He took me to the boutique in the hotel, and I picked out several pairs of cotton slacks, two blouses, a pair of overpriced sneakers, a pair of loafers, and underwear. I also bought a new red lipstick and a few other things I had done without for a long time. Then we went upstairs to our separate rooms, and I showered and napped.

Steven knocked on the door at about seven. We had never been intimate before, and here we were, alone in a hotel room. I was used to being around women of every shape and size, but sharing space with a man was very different—I didn't know how to react. I could feel my heart thumping. Interestingly, this was the first time in years my heartbeat speeded up not in anticipation of a prison fight but at the thought of being touched by those strong, expressive hands.

Steven knew I was nervous. He came over and sat next to me. For the longest time, all he did was rub my head and gently stroke my hair. My body relaxed, and I felt waves of pleasure from his simple, slow caresses. Finally, I twisted out of his grip and kissed him on the lips. When our tongues met, I felt giddy.

After more luscious, lingering kisses, Steven began to undress me. Though I had never been the most confident person about my body, I couldn't wait until we were both naked. We slipped under the thick, plush covers, but then he peeled them back to the foot of the bed so we could see each other. I felt as if I had never beheld a naked man before. Steven started talking softly to me, and to my complete amazement, I behaved as if another woman were inhabiting my body. I talked back, telling him how I had always loved his big, knowing hands. He told me how beautiful I looked and felt.

When we started to make love, he was deep inside me, and I had my arms on his shoulders, drawing him deeper. But instead of thrusting away like an oil well, Steven moved ever so slightly, so that our bodies stayed seamlessly joined. He whispered in my ear, "I want to be here awhile."

It seemed as if we rocked back and forth as one body for a

long time. Then Steven changed the pace and intensity, moving deeply inside me, pulled back, and grabbed my ass to pull me to him. I met him. We moved and bucked like some wild creature. My body took over as my mind and emotions rocketed into the stratosphere, on a tidal wave of pleasure and sensation more intense than anything I had ever known or thought possible. Then I felt Steven shudder, as if an earthquake had begun with him at its epicenter. Time ended, and we flew together.

Then another surprise. I guess I assumed he would be calm and tired and we would just lie there holding each other. Instead, Steven broke into paroxysms of laughter so infectious, I started laughing, too. We both laughed until it hurt; then, finally, we caught our breath and just lay there basking in each other's arms.

EPILOGUE

Tomorrow I will be fifty-nine years old. Except for some wrinkles around my eyes and cheeks, I look better then ever. Steven and I have been married for seventeen years. We talk all the time, laugh a lot, wrestle, ride horses, make love, and nap like a couple of geezers. When we need to argue, he lets me yell, I let him vent, and then we put it together. I cherish his love and so enjoy the feelings that come with loving him.

Our relationship was seeded when we prayed for my brother, Donny. Donny's death had left me with a deactivated heart and had also devastated Steven, his best friend. Once a year, out of love for Donny, we light a candle to celebrate his spirit. We do it with happiness because he is responsible for uniting us.

Shortly after arriving in Wyoming, Steven took me to the Wind River Reservation of the Shoshone and Arapaho peoples. I met alone with Eagle Heart for an hour before he walked me to his home to eat and celebrate with his family. Eagle Heart was fascinated by my prison experience. He listened with his eyes closed and then asked me questions. He wanted to know how I kept my spirit alive. When I told him about Doc and his words to me, Eagle Heart nodded gently.

I said, "You helped Steven in ways similar to how Doc helped me, didn't you?"

"I tried to influence Steven," he said. "When he returned from the war, he had the potential to turn bitter—many do. Some call that time 'the dark night of the soul.' I showed Steven how my people pray for the dead. We went together into the wilderness and honored with ritual those people he left behind. Together we built a sacred place for your brother. His death was a tremendous loss for Steven, and he needed to feel a connection to Donny's spirit. I watched Steven climb slowly out of the abyss he had fallen into."

"I will always love you for that, Eagle Heart," I said. "Thank you." I hugged him. He patted me on my neck and shoulders and said it was time to meet the family and eat.

I remember our wedding more for the surprise than for the actual marriage ceremony. Steven secretly bought round-trip tickets from San Francisco to Wyoming for June, Abel, and their son, William. Although we had spoken a few times, this would be our first in-the-flesh reunion.

June looked radiant. She came over to me, looked me up and down, and just whistled. "Damn, girl, love has transformed you." With this huge grin, she said, "Honey, I can't believe what a storybook life you're living. God is good to you. You've earned it."

We have visited June and her family every year since the wedding. The only time we missed was when my mother died. Our friendship has endured and always will endure.

Since leaving prison, I've learned many things. But the one lesson that eclipses all the others is really very simple, though not necessarily easy. If you get a second chance in life, grab it with all your strength and don't let go, don't turn back, don't hesitate. Take that second chance as if everything depended on it. Because it does.

CPSIA information can be obtained at www.ICGtesting.com
Printed in the USA
BVOW010611090112

279960BV00001B/11/P